THE
Linden
TREE

Also by Ellie Mathews

Ambassador to the Penguins

THE *Linden* TREE

Ellie Mathews

MILKWEED EDITIONS

© 2007, Text by Ellie Mathews
All rights reserved. Except for brief quotations in critical articles or reviews, no part of this book may be reproduced in any manner without prior written permission from the publisher: Milkweed Editions, 1011 Washington Avenue South, Suite 300, Minneapolis, Minnesota 55415, (800) 520-6455, www.milkweed.org

Published 2007 by Milkweed Editions
Printed in Canada
Cover design by Brad Norr
Cover photos: Corbis
Interior design by Dorie McClelland
The text of this book is set in Adobe Garamond Pro.
07 08 09 10 11 5 4 3 2 1
First Edition

Milkweed Editions specially thanks the Dougherty Family Foundation for its generous support of our children's book program.

Milkweed Editions, a nonprofit publisher, gratefully acknowledges sustaining support from Emilie and Henry Buchwald; the Bush Foundation; the Patrick and Aimee Butler Family Foundation; CarVal Investors; the Timothy and Tara Clark Family Charitable Fund; the Dougherty Family Foundation; the Ecolab Foundation; the General Mills Foundation; the Claire Giannini Fund; John and Joanne Gordon; William and Jeanne Grandy; the Jerome Foundation; Dorothy Kaplan Light and Ernest Light; Constance B. Kunin; Marshall BankFirst Corp.; Sanders and Tasha Marvin; the May Department Stores Company Foundation; the McKnight Foundation; a grant from the Minnesota State Arts Board, through an appropriation by the Minnesota State Legislature, a grant from the National Endowment for the Arts, and private funders; an award from the National Endowment for the Arts, which believes that a great nation deserves great art; the Navarre Corporation; Debbie Reynolds; the St. Paul Travelers Foundation; Ellen and Sheldon Sturgis; the Target Foundation; the Gertrude Sexton Thompson Charitable Trust (George R. A. Johnson, Trustee); the James R. Thorpe Foundation; the Toro Foundation; Moira and John Turner; United Parcel Service; Joanne and Phil Von Blon; Kathleen and Bill Wanner; Serene and Christopher Warren; the W. M. Foundation; and the Xcel Energy Foundation.

Library of Congress Cataloging-in-Publication Data

Mathews, Eleanor.
The linden tree / Ellie Mathews. — 1st ed.
        p. cm.
Summary: In 1948, nine-year-old Katy Sue's mother dies suddenly, and she and her family spend the next year trying to recover from their loss, assisted by her Aunt Katherine, who quit her teaching job to help out on their Iowa farm.
                ISBN-13: 978-1-57131-674-5 (pbk. : alk. paper)
                ISBN-10: 1-57131-674-4 (pbk. : alk. paper)
                ISBN-13: 978-1-57131-673-8 (hardcover : alk. paper)
                ISBN-10: 1-57131-673-6 (hardcover : alk. paper)
[1. Grief—Fiction. 2. Family life—Iowa—Fiction. 3. Farm life—Iowa—Fiction. 4. Aunts—Fiction. 5. Iowa—History—20th century—Fiction.] I. Title.
        PZ7.M49487Lin 2007
        [Fic]—dc22
2006038831

This book is printed on acid-free, recycled paper.

NATIONAL
ENDOWMENT
FOR THE ARTS
A great nation
deserves great art.

MINNESOTA
STATE ARTS BOARD

TO KAREN

THE
Linden
TREE

ONE

*I*f you go out our kitchen door, past the well, through the orchard, and toward the south end of our land, you can cross a grassy draw then go up a hill. There, you come to a big linden tree. That tree stands on its own bulge of ground. If you go up to it, you feel like its audience. Papa says it's older than all of us put together. Out there is where my mama is buried.

Under the linden tree is our closest point to heaven. If you stand there you can see our entire eighty acres. You can see how the upper pasture slants down to the pond and the wet spot alongside where the geese have trampled the grass to nearly nothing, and you can see over the top of the big barn and over the pig shed and the henhouse, being as how they are low, and then on to the cornfield and then our woodlot. You can see storms if they are coming, and to the west you can look toward town and sometimes see chimney smoke rising if the wind is right.

Turn around and you can see the county road that runs along the section line and whether anyone is headed our way, or if Mr. Culshank, our nearest neighbor, might be moving his tractor or farm equipment from one field to another, slowly bouncing along on his springy metal seat, maybe wiping his big face with a kerchief if the sun is high.

Ordinarily, here in Iowa, people are laid to rest in the churchyard. That's what the minister wanted Papa to agree to when Mama died. But town and the churchyard are three miles from here. Papa says this land is part of us and that Mama belongs on our land and that we should all be here forever and ever, one way or another.

Papa has a gentle manner but a stubborn one too. The minister knew better than to try to change my father's mind, but he tried anyway.

"I won't force the issue, Charles," the minister said. "It's just that nowadays—"

"Over here'd be just right," Papa said, gesturing across the ravine, "right over there, overlooking the house, don't you think?" His face was gray and blank. His eyes were two plain dots, flat and locked. People clustered around him saying how nice they thought the churchyard was. But Papa wasn't listening.

"Yes, yes," he said, "beautiful there. The churchyard.

Never miss a Sunday service. Now, as I was saying, we'll lay Edna right up there, don't you see?" He led the minister up our hill. Others followed behind. "Right under this great tree here is how I envision things. Don't you see?" He stopped abruptly and looked into one face after another, ending with the minister's. "Don't you see, Reverend? Right along here is where I want her to be."

Later on I went back to that spot. I sat on the grass alone. Then I noticed three men walking toward me up the rise. But it was only Papa and Ben and Uncle Dennis. They sat down on the grass, not saying anything at first, each listening to their own hard thoughts I suppose. Ben reached out to ruffle my hair but I ducked his hand.

Then Uncle Dennis got up and surveyed the old tree. It was just beginning to leaf out for spring.

"The roots'll be a tangle as far out from the trunk as those branches reach, y'know," he said. He looked up at the limbs then back at the ground where he pushed the toe of his boot at a clump.

"Papa," I said, "is Mama going to be—"

"But let's face it," my uncle interrupted, "we don't none of us have the gumption to snarl with any tangle of roots just now. This here's a huge tree. It'd take too much ax and hatchet work below the soil."

Ben had slipped away. "We could make it over here," he called out. He stood on open ground where the slope flattens toward the house. His mouth formed a thin, straight line around what he had said.

"That we could, son. That we could."

That's how it was decided. After the digging was done—and the digging took Uncle Dennis all afternoon and some of the next morning—people came from town and everywhere all around, hushed and stumbling. They made their way up the hill in twos and threes, wearing their church clothes to stand in clumps beneath the arms of our linden tree. The branches seemed to gather them in.

The air felt papery and dry that day. People touched my hair and face and smoothed the collar of my blue dress and said *poor thing* when they looked at me. Women hugged me to them, and I felt like a broken doll.

Our Aunt Katherine had arrived by train that morning, with two suitcases. She stood between my sister Ingrid and me while the minister said his words. Ingrid had her Bible held tight to her, and my aunt kept her arms around my shoulders all the while in case I crumpled. But I wasn't about to crumple. I knew if I did I would never be able to put the pieces of myself back together again. My brother Ben was fifteen then.

He stood across from us with some of the other men. Ben's face looked like glass that day, as if you could see into the working parts of him and see that they weren't moving very much at all. The sky pressed down and made my breathing feel hard.

Later, Papa put at the grave a thick oak board that he'd carved with his chisels. It says, "Edna, wife of Charles, mother of Benjamin, Ingrid, and Katherine"— that's me, the youngest, but everyone calls me Katy Sue to keep me straight from Aunt Katherine, who I was named for. Then, in bigger letters below all our Christian names, it says, "Hanson." Under that Papa carved Mama's birth date, October 3rd, 1912, and then March 24th, 1948, the day the meningitis took her away.

In Mama's family, there were two brothers, then Mama, then Aunt Katherine, then two more brothers.

Aunt Katherine had never married, maybe because she tended to be stern when things didn't go her way. She and Mama and the rest of the Gilberts came from over by Chesterton, in the eastern part of the state.

Aunt Katherine had always arrived by train for her summer visits. She'd have Mama laughing before they even left the station. Mama's laugh was like music. There had been times when I didn't think there could possibly be any more room for laughing in our house, but somehow Mama would be doubling over again and wiping at her eyes. Then August would come and it would be time for Aunt Katherine to straighten herself up and get back to Chesterton for the start of school. As a woman alone she kept herself going as a classroom teacher. She lived in rented rooms.

This time, even though Aunt Katherine was with us, the house was quiet.

With Mama gone and Ingrid being twelve going on thirteen, we knew most of the inside chores would be falling on her. I said I could take on the washing, but Papa wouldn't let me near the wringer. He said we'd had enough tragedy in the family already and that me getting my arm caught would just about do us in. If you ask me it was too hard for Ingrid to take on keeping the house and running the kitchen too, but she insisted. In any case, she never took the time to walk out to Mama's grave. I offered to go there with her, but she wouldn't hear of it. She didn't like to talk about Mama being gone and that was that.

I'm different from her. I say what's in my mind. I think about the past and how things used to be and who was here before us, like how that linden sapling must have looked once upon a time, skinny and alone up on the hill. I wonder where anyone found it and whether it was put in for a special time in someone else's family. I wonder if anyone pictured how important the tree would look some day.

That spring and after, I visited the linden tree when I wanted to remember how it was when we had Mama with us, how she smelled of lilacs after her bath and how she'd push her dark hair into waves while it was still wet, or how she'd wipe a wisp of it off her face when she was working hard at the stove.

They say the tree must have been planted by one of the men who homesteaded our farm. We have the papers that go with the land. Those first settlers were two brothers who cleared and plowed their places side by side. That was back when the government said if a family would work a square of land for a time and occupy it through the winters, they could have the acreage free and clear. My papa's people came along afterward and bought those two pieces together and planted corn and never left. Of course, Papa uses machinery, not a mule to work the fields the way those homesteaders did, but still, farming is a lot of work.

Everyone in our family is expected to pitch in to the best of our abilities. Because I was only ten years old then, I got some of the worst jobs, like thinning the lettuces. Those little leaves stuck to my fingers, and the soil was cold. That's how we made some of our money, though, selling from the garden, and someone had to tend to the cultivating and to the carrots and to encourage the pea vines onto their strings and the beans up their poles. Otherwise, there would be nothing to put out in our stand at the end of the road except eggs. I've almost always been the one to pick the strawberries and keep care of the chickens.

Of course, the farming didn't stop just because Mama was gone. We all had to continue as if everything was the same, but nothing was the same. Our house felt empty and muffled. It was as if we couldn't even see each other anymore, and it was almost as if we'd forgotten how to speak. Everyone has chores on a farm. Ben was tall enough to drive the tractor, and there was the harrowing to do and the heavy work in the barn like grinding the corn that I scatter in the yard for the hens.

Ingrid broke down more than any of us, although we all did our share. She was resigned to putting up the peas when their pods would plump up later in the season like Mama always had; she was capable of filling quart jars with whatever excess we had from the garden. In the evenings, though, she hardly ever joined the rest of us. Mostly, she sat beside the lamp and read stories. Sometimes she just sat and cried. None of us knew what to say to make her feel better.

It was strange. Even when Papa and Ben and Ingrid and I were in the same room, it felt as if each of us had been stranded on an island. My sister seemed so far away. I was scared. I was scared to have my mama gone. I cried too, like Ingrid, but I hid it. I had no idea what might happen to us next.

*M*ama had taken sick mighty fast. I remember Ingrid and me coming down our lane from the school bus that day. Halfway around the stand of willow trees we saw Papa pacing on the porch.

"Thank heavens you girls are home," he said, gathering us through the door. "Mama's been hit with a fever of some kind."

My sister and I threw our coats aside, rushed upstairs, and there she was in bed. Her eyes looked dark and wild and her cheeks were orangey red like a winter sunset. She turned to us and tried to smile but licked her lips instead.

"Ingrid," Papa said, "a little chamomile tea might ease the situation, if you would be so kind." He reached out and stroked Mama's forehead. I followed Ingrid to the kitchen, but before the water even had a chance to boil, Papa was back downstairs saying never mind about the tea. Instead, he went to our telephone between the kitchen and the parlor and lifted the earpiece.

"Operator?" he said, "I'd like to place a call to Dr. Winquist." He twisted the black cord that hung from the telephone. Then, as if suddenly jerked awake, he lurched, "Hello? Yes. Charles Hanson here. Yes, fine. No. It's Edna. Seems she has suddenly taken ill . . . no, not coughing . . . burning up with fever . . . a kind of pain—blue pain, she called it—right behind her eyes and I guess a pretty stiff neck . . . can't turn her head . . . I see . . . cold compresses? Good. Yes, I see. Bring her fever down."

He recradled the telephone and said to us in a rush, "You girls watch for the doctor. I'll be up in our room."

He grabbed a wet towel and took the stairs two at a time. Ingrid and I kneeled backward on the davenport with our arms folded across the top while we watched for Dr. Winquist's black Dodge. Instead, Ben came bursting through the kitchen door behind us. He'd taken the shortcut through the Culshanks' place and we didn't see him coming.

"Sh-h-h," Ingrid warned Ben.

"Yeah, be quiet," I added. "Mama's upstairs sick and Dr. Winquist is on his way right this minute."

"Shucks, I could have hitched a ride with the old guy," Ben grinned. "Instead, I had to walk all the way from Carson's corner." He broke off a chunk of leftover cake and popped it in his mouth.

"Benjamin," Ingrid said. "I'm telling you that Mama is sick."

"What's she got? A cold or something?"

Just then tires crunched the gravel in our driveway. "Oh, no!" I said, "We're supposed to be watching." I pulled Ingrid with me toward the front door.

The doctor's eyebrows connected into a single dark band across his face as he came up to our porch. "'Lo, girls," he said, and walked right past us and up the stairs carrying his black bag. There were no jokes from him that day. Ingrid and I followed. By then Ben had caught on that Papa would never take up anyone's time with something as silly as a cold.

The doctor is tall and can seem a little scary when he's with grown-ups. "'Lo, Charles," he said. He drew a chair up to the bed and lifted one of Mama's eyelids with his thumb. He asked her some questions in a low voice, but after a few she stopped answering.

"Mama?" Ben said in a gentle whisper. "Mama, we're here."

Ingrid and I watched all this from the doorway. Dr. Winquist had her stick her tongue out at him like how he had me do when I had the measles. He sat still a few minutes and watched her breathe without saying anything. He took a little bottle of something out of his black leather bag, looked at the writing on it, and put it back into its compartment. He picked up Mama's wrist and counted her pulse, then laid her hand back down and patted it. His eyebrows pulled together even more.

"Best thing, I'd say, is to let her sleep," he said. Then he glanced at us kids and said, "Charles? Maybe you and I could step outside for a minute to discuss how things might proceed."

They went to the porch and were gone for what seemed like a long time. Then I heard Papa crying out loud and saw the red glow of taillights fade out of our driveway. Papa came inside looking miserable. He lined us up on the davenport. "It seems Mama has a disease that might be stronger than she is." He cleared his throat. "The doctor says that we should make our peace with her." Ben made a funny noise in his throat and went straight outside.

It felt as if the room might be spinning. The roses on the parlor wallpaper looked like something I'd never seen before. I held my breath and tried to make myself believe that everything would probably be okay by morning as long as I did what I was told and didn't get in the way.

"Ingrid? Katy Sue?" Papa ruffled the silence. It seemed like hard work for him to say our names. They sounded as if they came from a place deep inside him that I'd never known about. "We need to be strong." The words came out like barbed wire. He fixed his eyes on us. "Get yourselves some bread and butter with hot milk, then put on your nighties and I'll come tuck you in when you're ready. Ben and I'll look after ourselves." The walls began to feel crooked and tipped. Mama was always the one who tucked us in.

He must have forgotten about tucking us in, though, because next thing I knew it was morning and time to get up. I crept barefoot down the hall and looked into their room. Mama hadn't moved. Papa sat beside her and nodded at me but didn't rise.

I remember how dust was blowing in from the cornfields when I went out for chores. Crows were squabbling in the upper pasture. The edge of the sky seemed too far away. It's funny how I remember exactly how everything was that day. I threw the scratch on the ground any old way. I was mad at the chickens for being how they always were, as if everything was okay.

Back inside Ingrid helped me with my hair. My sister had never done my braids before and it hurt when she combed the knots, but I didn't whine or complain. It wasn't the sort of day when anyone would be cross over something like that.

Of course Ben and Ingrid and I stayed home from school. We took turns being with Mama. She slept, mostly. One time in the afternoon, after Dr. Winquist came out a second time, she opened her eyes and turned their blueness straight on me.

"You're my littlest treasure," she said. Her voice was thin as a wire. I didn't know what to say back. I touched the cuff of her nightgown where the elastic was stitched on and squeezed my face shut as if that might make her disease go away. More than anything I didn't want her to know I was crying.

Mrs. Jessup brought food over. The Jessup place is where we've always bought our feeder pigs, so she came on in and made herself at home without asking.

"People make the mistake of not eating at a time like this, you know," she said, "but you've got to keep your appetites up now more than ever." She dabbed at a spot on the sink, "Now more than ever," she repeated quietly out the window, "no matter what comes our way." I half expected her to say *amen*. Then she snapped back to daylight, lifted a huge china dish of sausage and potatoes out of her basket, set it on the counter, and disappeared.

We weren't hungry, any of us. Her casserole turned cold and gummy right where she'd put it. It smelled as if it had onions in it, and the dish had a chip along the rim.

Night came on like a secret. I didn't think I'd ever

fall asleep, but next thing I knew Papa's hand was on my shoulder.

"Katy Sue," he said, "you'd best get up."

It was in the dark of the night. Ingrid and I followed him down the hall. Ben was already in there, sitting in the ladder-back chair next to the bed. He was still wearing his farm clothes. Mama was in her final sleep. I went up to the bed and touched the side of her face with the back of my fingers the way she always did to me when I was sick. Her face felt hot, and she didn't open her eyes at all. Then Ben took me onto his lap and held me tight under a quilt.

The sky began to come light in the east, and, as if that was more than she had strength for, Mama's breathing changed. After the breathing stopped for good, her skin took on the look of the candles she always bought us for Christmas Eve.

I didn't want to look at her but I couldn't help myself. I wanted my eyes shut tight against what was happening, but I couldn't keep from staring. Maybe we all felt like that, because eventually Papa lifted the bed-sheet and their blue comforter as if to cover her face, but then he stopped halfway and folded the blankets back. "I don't guess you'll mind if we look at you just a little while longer, Edna," he whispered. He kissed her forehead and invited the three of us to do the same.

Her skin was warm under my lips and her hair smelled salty in a good way.

None of us around the bed made a sound for a long time. Everything went quiet and motionless like floating. We just looked at her, because it didn't seem real. And the sun came in the window as if nothing had happened at all.

THREE

In the days that followed the funeral, Ingrid was determined to keep things in the kitchen the way they'd always been, even with Aunt Katherine staying with us. Still and all, Ingrid was only twelve years old. She didn't know everything there was to know about cleaning a chicken or boiling bones for soup. Aunt Katherine came down one morning after Ingrid had burned her finger on hot bacon grease.

"You should have called your papa or me if this big old iron pan was too heavy for you to drain the fat," Aunt Katherine said.

"I can do it." Ingrid's jaw was set. In the meantime, some of the grease had spilled onto the hot part of the stove and was smoking up the whole house.

"Mama lets us help with the cooking," I said.

"Helping when it's fun is one thing," Aunt Katherine said, "doing things beyond your capacity is another. You mustn't put yourself or others at risk." She caught herself and put her palm to her forehead. "Oh, good lord, what am I saying? I'm not here to scold you." She looked out the window. "It's just that—I don't know—I remember how she and I—when we were young like you—" She swallowed hard and turned back to us. "Did she ever tell you about the time—?" For a moment everything in the room seemed to freeze. Then her voice came like a dry summer wind, "Well, we burned our fingers too." She looked back to the window. "I just can't believe she's gone," she whispered to herself.

But the incident wasn't over. Ingrid had been sucking on the knuckle she'd burned. She jerked her hand out of her mouth and blurted, "I can do anything our Mama did!" Her eyes were two glowing coals. Ingrid shouted again, "I *can!*" and she stormed upstairs. Most times, no one in our family shouted, particularly not at each other.

Aunt Katherine pulled one of the oak chairs out from the table and sank down. She gestured for me to come onto her lap. I wavered. I wanted the hug, but it would have felt disloyal to Ingrid, who was upstairs wailing.

"I'll just be over here," I said, pulling out the chair opposite. I wasn't sure what to do or say next. It wasn't as if we were fixing to have a tea party with the gold-painted cups or anything. It was only nine o'clock in the morning. The pendulum clock ticked.

Our kitchen has two stoves, the big old black one near the door and a white one in the corner that runs on electricity. Mama had ordered the white one from the catalog two years before, but that one she used mostly in the summer. Electricity didn't grow on trees, after all, she used to say. The big iron black one is the kind you make a fire in, and we usually have plenty of stove wood from whatever blows down on the far side of our pond every winter.

"I can't stay here with you forever, you know," said Aunt Katherine. "I told your papa I'd see the family through till you start back to school. Then I have my own school to return to."

"Yes, ma'am, I know."

"I'm thinking by Monday you might be ready. They say waiting doesn't make it any easier."

"Yes, ma'am. My teacher, Mrs. Breton, said the same at the funeral."

"I know Ben wants to get back to his studies. And Ingrid would benefit from getting outside herself, don't you think? I'm sure people will show every kindness."

"We'll be okay," I said. I had already begun to wonder how we could possibly manage on our own. I didn't want to think about getting ready for school in the morning without Mama to help with my hair and pack my lunch and remind me when to leave for the bus. I didn't dare think about Aunt Katherine leaving us alone with the house feeling hollow and strange.

"But for now," Aunt Katherine said, "why don't you fetch your sister from upstairs. You and she can help me organize these pans and dishes to return. This blue platter is Eva Culshank's, isn't it?"

"It's Ida Culshank," I said.

"What?"

"Mrs. Culshank's given name is Ida," I said. "Not Eva."

"Oh," Aunt Katherine said. "I thought it was Eva," and she gave me a look that made me feel small. "Well, anyway. I thought we might all three walk over, being as how they're so close by."

Neighbors had brought cooked chickens and home-made cottage cheese and sticky buns to set out for well-wishers. To me, it had all tasted like dust. By now plates had been washed and stacked on the cabinet by the kitchen door.

Aunt Katherine continued, "Your papa said he could drive us to town this afternoon. We can start to take some of these other things back to their owners."

None of us had left the house for a week. I liked the idea of going to town. At the same time I feared anyone asking me how I was getting on. The wrong kind of gentle question could make me cry, and I was determined not to let anyone see me cry. Not Ingrid. Not Papa. Not Ben. Not even Aunt Katherine. But especially no one in town.

Mama had once said it was a sign of strength not to cry over everything that came along. More than that, though, I was afraid. The sobs that wanted to escape my throat might never stop if they started. The hole inside me had no bottom, no top, no edges of any kind. I wasn't about to let myself fall into a pit like that.

Ingrid agreed to ride along to town, although she wasn't particularly good company. Her presence felt like a blank page. She wouldn't talk about what she was thinking or feeling. I don't know why, but I could scarcely *stop* talking.

"Papa," I said on our way home, "who planted that linden tree, anyway?"

"You know the answer to that," he said. "It was the homesteaders who first worked our land."

"But do you think they got it as a skinny little sapling and left it alone up on our hill?"

"I don't know, Katy Sue. I couldn't say."

"But, Papa, do you think they pictured how it would look after it spread wide?"

Ingrid said, "Quit your yammering. Did it ever occur to you Papa might want to drive in peace and quiet?"

"But, Papa—" I started more quietly, "do you

think—" I looked sideways at my sister, who seemed to be monitoring our conversation. "Never mind," I said. But I wondered whether those homesteaders would feel okay knowing that our mama was up there with the tree they'd planted.

Once home from town, Papa headed for the barn with Ben. Ingrid and Aunt Katherine went inside to see about supper. That left me free to wander down to the orchard. I didn't have to ask who'd planted those trees: my grandpa. Peaches, apples, and pears. He'd laid them out like a marching band. The cherry trees he'd planted by the house where the petals fall on the walk every spring. I thought the blossoms looked like girls' party dresses.

I sat in the orchard on an overturned cider pail, feeling small. Just then, out of the corner of my eye, something moved across the clouds. For a split second it seemed as if Mama was starting toward me from behind the Gravenstein tree, maybe about to call to me or say it was time to wash up for supper. In reality it was only the shadow of a crow. For that little dart of time, though, it seemed like the most natural thing in the world for me to see her in the orchard. Like the thousand times it had actually happened.

The crow landed on a broken branch and hunched its shoulders. I sank back. I couldn't make myself believe I'd never see my mama or hear her voice in the orchard again.

Eventually Ben came looking for me. "C'mon," he said, "we've got time to work in the garden before supper. Things have fallen behind with—you know." I automatically took his outstretched hand. I couldn't remember the last time we'd walked hand in hand. His fingers felt warm and tight around mine.

"What were you doing down here anyway?" Ben asked. "I looked all over for you."

Instead of answering I let my hand go limp and drop out of his. He nudged me with his elbow. "Last one there's a rotten egg," he said, trying to sound jolly. But I didn't fall for it. He broke into a half run, but I didn't fall for that either.

Inside the garden fence, Ben crouched at a row of lettuce seedlings. "Take out all the ones closer than an inch apart," he said. "Leave the biggest."

"Don't tell me how to do what I already know how to do," I said. I didn't mean to sound so cross, but what did he think I was—a baby?

FOUR

*I*f someone had cut off one of my legs and then told me to walk, it would have been easier than going back to school. As it was, we stumbled around in a blur. My legs were still there but they felt like sticks of firewood. People came and went from our house. Mrs. Cassidy had even done our washing and hung it to dry. But the morning chores were still ours.

Everything looked like dirt and felt like cotton, even the cold handle of the pump when I went to fill the calves' watering trough by the fence. Crows pestered around in the upper pasture. They made ugly, skritchy noises that sounded like black strings tossed into the wind. But somehow we kept the farm going.

I remember being in the henhouse the first morning after Aunt Katherine left on the train. Ingrid had gotten up at five thirty to fix griddle cakes and get ready for school. I was filling the hens' watering jar when I heard Ben with our two Jersey cows, Daphne and Emeline. Time was short before the bus was due.

"Get in there," my brother's voice came through the barn wall. "Get over here you big—" Then I heard what sounded like Ben striking one of the cows' big warm sides. The sound of that slap made me jump; I'd never known anyone in our family to be rough with our animals. The cows thudded their hard feet on the wooden barn floor as they lurched into their stalls to be milked, mooing and bellowing for their hay. Then Papa's voice rose above Ben's and Ben no longer sounded so angry with Daphne and Emeline, and I heard the *tshh-tshh-tshh* of milk hitting the bottom of the pails.

My teacher for that year, Mrs. Breton, who also goes to our church, had been at the funeral. Maybe she'd been right when she advised Papa that the longer we waited to return to school, the harder it would be to start again. It had been only a week and a half, but it seemed like a month.

Papa hacked up some leftover pot roast from the Cassidys for sandwiches that he threw into our lunch pails. Then it was rush and hurry to get to the end of our lane in time to see the yellow bus coming around the corner on the county road. Ingrid climbed on ahead of me. Everybody looked at us and hushed. I felt conspicuous. Wayne Kirkpatrick, who'd sat in the very front seat every single morning since the start of the year and who always, always stuck his foot out in the aisle for me to trip over, got up from his seat to make a place. Alma Lorrington left off with Sherry Davis and came up to sit beside me. She touched my hand with hers. I didn't have to say a word.

Our school is yellow brick, with swings and monkey bars, and a baseball field to the north. The buses stop on the south, opposite the play shed. That's where kids take their balls and hopscotch chalk and jump ropes when the weather's bad.

Mrs. Breton was at her desk when we went into the classroom. Deep down I was glad I had the strictest teacher in the whole school. My biggest fear was that I would start to cry in front of the other kids. Any unexpected kindness might cause me to break down, and I was certain Mrs. Breton wouldn't be inclined to speak softly or single me out. She never had.

But I was wrong. At morning recess she asked me to stay behind. I was hoping with all my might that she only wanted to talk about the lessons I'd missed. I was pretty sure nothing sweet or sad would be said. But I was wrong about that too.

Half sitting on her teacher's desk, Mrs. Breton removed her glasses. I'd never seen her without them. She's older, so sometimes her eyes were sort of watery looking. But that day her eyes looked nice, not at all stern. She looked at me and tried to smile.

"Things going as well as can be expected out at your place?" she asked.

"Fine, I guess," I said.

"Everyone sleeping okay?"

"I guess so," I lied. I lined up my two pencils with each other in the groove at the top of my desk.

"I suppose it's hard coming back here."

"No ma'am." I darted a glance at Mrs. Breton's face. "Well, Ingrid said it was hard. She cries all the time."

"Oh?"

"And has outbursts. She says our aunt is going to try to take over."

"Oh. Is your aunt still with you?"

"No, ma'am. She left on the train. But Ingrid says she'll be back."

"I had a nice exchange with her," Mrs. Breton said. She edged up with her teacher's chair close to my desk by the windows in the third row. "Sometimes it helps to talk things out, you know." I felt her eyes drilling into me and I didn't know what to say, so I ran my finger along a place where someone had carved a zigzag in the top of my desk a long time ago.

"Your aunt looks a lot like your mama, doesn't she?" Mrs. Breton said. All of a sudden she was sounding uncommonly gentle, considering how quickly she could turn on any kid who so much as fidgeted in class.

"Yes, ma'am," I said, even though I felt insulted having to agree that anyone looked like my mama.

"People say it was meningitis your mother had."

"I guess so, ma'am. The kind they don't have pills for."

"I lost a baby daughter, years ago."

"You did?" I tried to picture Mrs. Breton with her own baby.

"Yes. She had influenza. There was nothing anyone could do."

"Then that makes you and me criss-crossed in a way. You with your daughter and me with my mother."

"Yes, I guess it does," she said. She leaned across and tucked one of my braids behind my shoulder.

I left off tracing my finger over the zigzag on my desk and looked up. Mrs. Breton had wisps of hair straggling around her face and coming out of the pins she used to hold her bun in place. She was not a fat woman, but bigger than most and with a wide face and a wider lap. For a moment her gray woolen skirt looked like an inviting place to climb onto, but, of course, I inched away.

"I tried to draw a picture of her," I said, but immediately regretted blurting that out.

"That would be one way to keep hold of your memories."

"I was afraid I'd forget what she looked like."

"Oh, I doubt that will happen," Mrs. Breton said, in a way that sounded warm and good, and I began to feel ashamed for ever having joined in with other kids snickering about her behind her back.

I didn't know what to do next. I went back to my two pencils, turning them to where their two points were touching. I made them line up perfectly straight with each other.

"I knew your mama, you know."

"Yes, ma'am," I said, and without warning my breath started coming in sawtooth jerks.

"She was a lovely woman."

For a minute I felt as if I were floating, like when Ben had held me under the quilt. My mama's face was the most beautiful in the world. Without my sensing them coming, my tears began to leak. One dribbled off my chin and soaked into the cloth of my cotton skirt, leaving a dark splotch on the blue print. Mrs. Breton squeezed one of my hands, which made some of the hurt go deeper and go away all at once.

"Her skin was like fine china, wasn't it?"

"Papa said she was the prettiest girl in Iowa," I tried to say, but all I could make was a whisper.

For a long time neither of us spoke. Then I dared to look up. "Mrs. Breton?"

"What is it, dear?"

"If I told you something, would you not laugh at me?"

"You have my word."

"There's something I didn't tell my mama. When she was sick, I mean." Mrs. Breton leaned forward. I bunched my fingers into the splotches in my skirt. "Mama said I was her special treasure and I didn't answer." I twisted my fingers in my skirt as if to make the wet spots disappear. "I should have. But I didn't know what to say." I had nowhere to look but into my own lap. "I mean—I didn't think—I didn't think she would really—that she'd really *die*." My hands stopped moving. "I thought I had time to say it, you know, *later*."

"And now there is no later, is there? That's the heartbreak." Mrs. Breton touched my wrist and said in a voice that made me think of the warmest, deepest, clearest pool imaginable, "You wanted to say how much you loved her, didn't you?"

I snapped my eyes to Mrs. Breton's. "How did you know?"

"But hadn't you ever told her that?"

"Oh, yes, ma'am. Lots of times. All the time. Every *day*. She was the best mama anyone ever had."

"Then you didn't have to tell her again. She already knew. You have nothing to worry about. Nothing at all. There's more to loving someone than what you say to them, you know."

"Yes, ma'am," I said. "But still, I wish I'd said it."

"I'll tell you what. Why don't you find something around your farm to draw some pictures of. Then you can put her in the pictures. Just the way you want to see her. You have milk cows out at your place, don't you?"

"Some days it seems we're raising nothing but crows out in the field."

"Then draw me some crows."

"I don't like crows."

"Well, okay."

I couldn't have said why, but that made me laugh on top of my crying, thinking of crows at a time like that and because people sort of teased Mrs. Breton about how serious she could be about drawing pictures all the time, and there we were talking about crows.

"Maybe I might be able to draw a better picture of the chickens," I said. "Most days, I talk to the chickens when I let them out."

"Chickens would be a fine thing to draw," Mrs. Breton said.

I hadn't meant to tell so much to anyone, but once it was out of my mouth, I couldn't take it back. By then I could hear kids outside starting to line up with the playground monitor to come inside. Mrs. Breton straightened herself and offered me her handkerchief, but I had my own hankie in my lunch pail.

"I hope you'll feel free to come to me," she said.

"Yes, ma'am, I expect I will."

"And I hope you know how sorry I am for your loss."

"Yes, ma'am, I know." And I did somehow know.

Recess was over. I sat up straighter at my desk as kids burst through the door. I didn't know why, but I felt a little bit more like part of the class again.

❧

Knowing my teacher was on my side, I wanted to please her. Later in the week, I asked Ben one afternoon, "Do you think it's hard to draw pictures of crows?"

"I dunno."

"But all you'd be using would be the black crayon."

"Put 'em on the green pasture," he said. "Make the sky blue."

"If I were to make a drawing of our family, should I still have Mama be in the picture?"

"Why wouldn't you?" he said. "She'll always be our mama."

That was a comfort. I went off to a corner of the barn where the sun streamed in the window. I had paper and crayons, and I tried to think of how our family might look if we were still the way we were meant to be. I put Papa up on the porch and Ingrid and Ben by the cherry tree. I drew the cherry tree in bloom, because I had one crayon that was just right for the petals. I colored it in with lots of pink curly lines. I drew Mama in and colored her brown hair, but it didn't look as shiny as it should have. My hand shook when I put Mama in the picture. I put roses in her cheeks, but I drew a tear under one of Papa's eyes. Then I colored in our roof, which is red, but the red crayon was too bright and it sort of ruined the picture. I was sad about that. Then I realized that I hadn't put myself in anywhere, but by then I'd put in all the grass and sky and everything around the edges and there was no room to add myself. I decided Mrs. Breton would understand. Before I finished, I drew a yellow box around Mama, because I was starting to realize that none of us would be able to touch her anymore.

FIVE

*D*ays later Ingrid and I came in from the school bus and found Papa in the kitchen. It was rare to find him inside during the afternoon, but there he was.

"Look here at this!" he said, thumping his finger on a typewritten letter lying on the kitchen table.

Ingrid picked it up. "It's from Jake's museum," she said. There was a dinosaur skeleton printed at the top of the page.

"You bet it is," Papa said. "And he's coming out for a visit. Going to be here in five days!"

A visit from Papa's best friend would be different from those of all the other men and women who'd brought their long faces out to our place. Callers didn't dare utter Mama's name for fear of upsetting us. When we were alone, though, we said her name all the time. We talked about her and told stories about her and remembered how patient she was when we wanted to play Parcheesi.

I took a deep breath and asked Papa, "Does Jake know about—"

"Yes, Katy Sue. He's been informed."

"Read it yourself," Ingrid shoved the letter at me. "It starts right out saying, 'With Edna gone—'"

But I didn't want to read the letter. I wanted to dance around the kitchen with Papa.

All in all, we'd already had more company than we knew what to do with. The weather had grown warm and the flies weren't too bad, so most callers were invited to the chairs on our front porch. No one knew what to say after the pleasantries were finished, though. I'd sit on the steps and watch those grown-ups fidget while they asked about our crops or whether the soil had warmed up enough to germinate our corn. Mrs. Garrison had come out two Sundays in a row. She's a World War II widow; her husband died on some island or other in the Pacific Ocean. She acted as if she knew all about our situation and how we felt. But she did not.

It wasn't only people from nearby farms who took pity on us. Uncle Dennis, Papa's brother, came to help stretch new fence wire on its posts one day. Aunt Rosa always used to be too busy with their own place twenty miles across the county to ride along, but she came that day, and she brought my cousins Francine and Betsy, who are younger than Ingrid and me and who always get in our hair no matter what.

But a visit from Jake would be different. He wouldn't chirp and cluck like the ladies from church. His bright face would help us get outside our sorrow and feel the sun on our skin again.

His real name is Hamilton Jacobs, but no one calls him by his first name, and we're allowed to call him Jake along with everybody else. He's exactly Papa's age. He lives in the East now, but was at one time from around here, having graduated from the high school with Papa. Then Jake went off to Iowa's state college and studied some more subjects. Papa calls Jake a sheepskin man, being as he earned a diploma. After his schooling, he moved away from these parts to get work at a big museum. His people are gone, but he stays in touch because he and Papa have always been friends and always will be. Jake feels more like an uncle than some of our real uncles.

It was a hard wait, but finally the day came when Ingrid and I arrived home and saw Jake's gray Nash automobile parked next to the barn. Ingrid threw her school things aside and got the first hug.

But mine was longer. He didn't swing me around

in the air the way he usually did when I was little. Instead, he took my face in both of his hands and looked at me hard.

"Hullo there, little Katydid," he said, and ran one thumb across my cheek. "I won't ask how you've been."

I sniffled.

"None of it seems fair, what's happened here, does it?"

His softness broke me down. I flung my arms around his waist and let my tears soak into his sweater. Then I felt Papa's hand gentle on the top of my head. He said, "We'd best let our friend bring his things into the house, don't you think? There'll be time for more hugs later."

Jake had driven all the way from New York City, stopping along the way here and there to look at birds or foxes or even snakes. The trunk of his car was packed full of cameras and what he called museum specimen jars. He had supplies for sleeping out and a little burner to heat his food with. The seats in his Nash folded down to make a bed. He wasn't the sort to rent a hotel room if he didn't have to, even though his museum would pay for it.

We took Jake in through our front door, which we hardly ever use, because hardly anyone goes into our parlor. The furniture there is slippery and not very comfortable to sit on. Jake looked around. The wallpaper has roses on it and the rug has roses, too, but they have faded where the sun touches. The window shades were pulled down.

We walked him straight through to the kitchen. The walls in there are the color of sunlight and the tin cabinets are painted white. The stove was warm with a low fire inside to keep Papa's coffeepot warm.

Jake looked around. "Nothing's changed since the last time," he said, "except, of course—" and ran his hand along the top of the wooden table where we eat our meals.

We showed him to our spare room downstairs, next to the bathroom. He touched the blue quilt that Mama had pieced when we were all little. "I remember this," he said. "I think one of these little squares used to be an old shirttail of mine," and he turned back a corner of the quilt as if he might recognize a patch of cloth.

Upstairs is where our family sleeps. The hall there is papered with ivy leaves that match the green of our shutters. On the outside, our house is white.

"C'mon kids," Papa said. He shooed us out the door. "Let's give Jake a chance to settle in."

Jake had already been planning to head out West when he received word about Mama. Right away he changed the time of his trip so he could visit. After he left our place he would take photographs of sandhill cranes in their summer nests.

Jake hung up his clothes in our closet and brought out a *National Geographic* magazine. He showed us pictures of what those big birds look like, and he made the sound of their call way down deep in his throat. Ingrid laughed and said it sounded as if he needed a doctor. I think that might have been the first time Ingrid had laughed since the funeral. I was afraid she'd catch herself, as if it were somehow improper to have a good time if your mother was gone, but she didn't and I was glad, although just thinking about it almost made me cry again.

Jake assured us his cranes could wait and that he wouldn't have to rush off. He picked up the end of one of my braids and tickled my neck with it. Then he sat back with his eyes steady on my face. "You look a powerful lot like her, don't you?" he said. With that he closed his magazine and ran his thumb along the edge of its pages a couple of times. He turned to Papa, shook his head, and said, "Personally, I don't know how you're getting from one day to the next."

"Yup," said Papa.

"Think I'll walk some of that four-day drive out of my bones if you don't mind me excusing myself."

"The grave's up by that linden tree on the hill," Papa said.

Jake went back into the spare room, picked up his Bible, and slipped through the kitchen door. The corner of our kitchen has a grandfather clock that Papa winds every Saturday. Being Thursday, the weights were low on their chains. The pendulum swung like always. Ingrid nudged me.

"I'm fixing sausages and beans for supper," she said. "Go down and get us a jar of stewed tomatoes, and I'll make a batch of biscuits to go along."

Ben and Papa were doing chores by the time Jake came back in. He sat at the table and took out a little book that he always carried around with him, a book with nothing printed on the pages. He wrote something down. Whenever Jake had an idea or saw something interesting, he'd pull that book out of his shirt pocket and use his blue fountain pen to write or to draw little pictures on those pages. Finally, he tucked the little book back into his pocket.

"Ingrid," he said, "I brought you something." He caught my eye. "There's one for you, too, Katydid," and he placed the second of two clamshells on the middle of the table. Each had a thin strip of green tissue paper holding it closed, as if the clam was still living inside.

"Are these from the ocean?" I said, and started to grab for mine.

"Hold on," Jake stilled my hand. "Ingrid? Leave off those biscuits for thirty seconds, why don't you, and Katy Sue, rinse out that tomato jar over there and bring it to me full of water. These shells came all the way from Japan. They have something special inside."

Our sink is in the corner. Above it is a big window that faces our hill. As I waited for the jar to fill, I stood on my tiptoes to see through the glass, glancing outside as if to tell Mama that something fun was coming up.

First Ingrid dropped her shell into the jar of water, then I dropped mine. Next thing we knew, the strips of paper soaked through and gave way. The shells opened up and out came all kinds of colored paper flowers, reaching for the surface. A sea garden. The flowers were anchored to the shells with green threads that looked like stems, and we put the jar on the windowsill above the sink. Jake says you can get absolutely anything you can imagine back East.

When Ben came in, Jake gave him two postcards from his museum. One showed a penguin with orange patches on the sides of its head; the other showed different animal skulls all the way from a mouse's to a coyote's.

Ingrid and I got supper on the table. Once we all

sat down, Papa said, "Jake? I suppose you could do the honors." I bowed my head for the saying of the grace.

"Dear Lord," Jake said, in a soft voice like he'd use to call some special bird, "You have already blessed this land. Now, we ask that You bless this food and those who've raised it. Bless these young cooks and the woman who taught them. Our hearts ache with Edna gone. Bless her soul, and help us find our way again. Amen."

The rest of us said, "Amen." Ben cleared his throat, and Papa said quietly, "She was a good woman."

SIX

*T*he second night of Jake's visit was a Friday. Ingrid kept me out of the kitchen, as if she was fixing to make some sort of surprise. I didn't see what the big deal was. All I saw was a dumb old pot of stew with carrots and potatoes.

Supper was quiet that night, with just the clinking of the plates and the dishing up, until Ingrid's hand flew to her mouth. "Oh, no," she blurted out, "the butterscotch cake!" She leapt from the table, knocking her chair askew. Until she started carrying on, nobody had noticed that thick smoke was leaking out all around the oven door, which had turned black where it ought to have been white. "The cake. I forgot about the cake," she said. Then Papa got up, too, knocking his chair clean over. I smelled fire. I didn't even know she had made a cake. It was a kind Mama used to make for special occasions. After she put the icing on she used to stick it back in the oven, under the broiler, to melt the sugar.

The flames were little and they went right out. Papa

and Ben went after them with a wet dish towel. Our back porch is screened all around and it's a good place to cool a pie or anything from the oven. Jake carried the pan out there to let it finish its stinking and fuming. Ingrid went upstairs, crying.

"Go after your sister," Papa said to me. He sounded gentle and kind, like it wasn't a time for anyone to shout. Even the biggest, fattest, sweetest butterscotch cake with coconut icing is gone as soon as you eat it. But feelings last.

"It's not her fault," Papa went on. I didn't move. My sister is more than two years older than me. How could I offer comfort? "Go on, Katy Sue. Tell her it's not so bad and that we all want to finish our meal together." He used that tone that makes me want to do exactly as he says, so I started for the door. He righted his chair and took his seat. As I went down the hall, I overheard him say to Jake, "I expect Edna would have a fit to see the oven like this. Let's hope she's looking down on another part of the county right now."

"Tell Ingrid I'll take everyone to the creamery after we tidy up, Katy Sue," Jake called after me. He'd joined Papa and Ben back at the table. "My treat," he called again, "butter brickle all around."

I climbed the stairs to our room. Ingrid was on her bed whimpering.

I tried to sound like Mama when she handled a situation like that, but I didn't feel any strength in myself to coax Ingrid back downstairs. On the other hand I knew I had to, because in our family we didn't like to leave troubles dangling.

"Don't cry over spilt milk," I said.

"It's not about milk, stupid. It was a cake."

"I bet you put some milk into the batter, though—" I didn't care that she called me stupid. I just wanted to get her to stop crying. I had to.

"Buttermilk," she said. "Two cups."

"Jake says we can go to the creamery for dessert. Butter brickle."

Ingrid looked up. "He did?"

"Well, you probably wouldn't have to have butter brickle if you wanted to choose some other flavor."

I dared to sit on my sister's bed, something she would have ordinarily complained about. I said, "Come on, Ingrid. Everybody makes mistakes. You know that. We'd rather have you at the table than fussing over a burnt cake."

I was surprised when Ingrid began drying her eyes. Had my comforting helped or was it Jake's offer of ice cream? Whatever it was, she followed me downstairs and we picked up the pieces of dinner. Ben cleaned the soot off the cake pan to where it looked better than new. We rode to town in Jake's Nash, with the three of us kids in the back.

Ben said it used to be that if you wanted ice cream, the only choice was to crank your own. We Hansons know how to do that. It takes forever, though, and after the cranking you have to let it sit in the freezer for a time before it's good and ready. By then you might not even want ice cream anymore.

At Jackson's they have a big window where you can look in and see all the flavors in their cartons. Ben had a double scoop of chocolate. Ingrid had the peach. Jake asked for butter pecan, as they were fresh out of brickle. Nobody would tell me what a brickle was; they just laughed when I asked. I had strawberry, which Papa had to finish half of, and that was on top of the scoop of peppermint stick he'd already licked up.

On the way home, with my tummy feeling that it would burst, Jake suddenly jerked the steering wheel and made the car swerve. A pheasant had run in front of the car. That got Papa and Jake swapping stories about the old days, when they used to go out and hunt grouse and pheasant along the drainage ditches.

"With you loving birds so dang much," Papa said, "do you still shoot any?"

"'Course I do. You can study 'em dead or alive for different purposes. You can be darn sure, though, that they're all dead before we stuff 'em for the museum," Jake said. "And some of them have got to be shot to get 'em into that condition."

"Even the itty-bitty ones? They don't get tore up by the bullets?" Papa said.

"For them we use an itty-bitty rifle." Jake said. "You don't go after a wren with a thirty-aught-six."

"Ever shot a crow?" Papa asked.

"You can't shoot crows. I don't care how good a shot you are or how many you've got in a field. Bullets'll just go thunk-thunk-thunk all around 'em. No one can shoot a crow." I could tell it was a joke between them from a time way back.

"I'll wager you," Papa said with a wink. I knew for a fact that my Papa had hit a crow a time or two when they pestered around the crops, and I expected that Mr. Jacobs knew which end of a rifle was which, only neither of them let on.

"I'll tell you one thing, though," Jake said, "if ever you do get a crow, you'll want to hang it from a fence post for all the others to see. Supposed to teach 'em a lesson. 'Least that's what my dad always claimed. And he was a pretty astute farmer if I do say so. Maybe just an old wives' tale, but that's what he said."

"I'll wager you on the crow," Papa said.

"Oh, yeah? How much?"

"There's, oh, I don't know," he turned to us in the backseat, "what d'ya think, kids? Four bits?" He turned to Jake. "There's half a dollar in it for you if you can bag a crow before you leave our place." Jake whistled one low note like it was the offer of a lifetime. "On the other hand," Papa said, "if I nail one first, you'll have to stuff it for me with that little kit you have in the back of this car."

"Deal's on," said Jake, and he took his hand off the steering wheel to shake on it.

SEVEN

*P*apa's wager hung in the air. With Jake knowing so much about crows and cranes, it struck me that he could help with my picture for Mrs. Breton. When he'd first arrived, he set a little box of watercolors on the dresser in his room. Later, he showed me how he used those paints. He hardly needed to touch the brush on the little pot of blue to make the sky look right for a sketch he'd made in his little book. Jake knew how to do all sorts of things. Drawing a bunch of skritchy old crows was practically his specialty.

School hadn't let out yet, but I went outdoors every chance I got. Jake took me around with him and told me the names of all the different plants that were appearing in our woodlot, and we went to the pond to see how close to being frogs our tadpoles were. It felt as if time had stretched itself out, and suddenly we had the warmth and light to do all the things we couldn't do when winter had cooped us up.

Afternoons grew hot. In other years Papa might have taken us to Lake Augusta to cool off, but between having a visitor and not being in the mood for a family outing, nobody talked about going swimming. Besides, Mama had always made our picnics.

The quarry is closer than Lake Augusta, and some kids go there to swim. Everyone knows that place is dangerous, but older boys go there anyway. Papa has always forbidden any of us to swim at the quarry.

It felt especially hot that afternoon when the Wilcox boys came by. The Wilcoxes live past the Culshanks about a mile. They picked Ben up in their old Ford, an hour before the evening chores. He climbed in and away they went. He was old enough to go off with them like that without asking permission. Still, it made me nervous to watch. You never knew what Brad and Nolan Wilcox would be up to. Their family didn't seem to have as many rules as ours. You'd think they'd have more, given that there are nine kids.

It was plain as day when they came back an hour later that they'd all been swimming, and there hadn't been time to go all the way to Lake Augusta. The crown of Ben's brown hair was still wet when they dropped him off. Not only was Ben late, but Daphne and Emeline were stomping and bellowing, with their udders full.

I was playing with our calico cat in the shadow of the cherry trees. Papa took a long look at Ben, who was standing between the house and the barn. He's not the sort to thrash us kids when we misbehave. He does something worse. He gets quiet. He tells us he's disappointed, and he looks at us hard until we squirm.

"You went with those Wilcox boys, did you?" Papa said. He sounded casual to start.

"Yes, sir," said Ben.

"Down there to the quarry?"

"Yes, sir. I did."

"Swimming in the quarry, were you?"

"Well, sir, let me—" Ben began.

Papa cut him off with a hand locked onto one of Ben's shoulders and looked at him severely. "Now, Benjamin," Papa said—and by using his full name I knew he was really angry—"Benjamin, let's give you one more chance with that question: Did you go swimming in the *quarry*?"

Ben scuffed his toe around in the dirt and didn't look up. "I guess I did, sir. A little bit."

"You guess so." Papa released him. "You guess so." I didn't know what Papa would do to Ben. The cows were kicking up a fuss, stomping and carrying on in their stanchions. They'll go in there of their own accord come milking time; and wait to be locked in at their feeding trough. I knew they were standing there, cranky and fussed.

"Do you remember how the Tuttle boy lost the use of his limbs there, diving into that rock overhang an' breaking his neck and all?" Papa asked. He and Ben hadn't moved one inch toward the barn, and I could see it made Ben nervous that Daphne and Emeline were waiting on him.

"Yes, sir. I do," Ben said. He was looking to the side and off to the horizon and back toward the barn. Anywhere but look at Papa. "But I didn't dive," Ben said, so quietly that I almost couldn't hear him.

"What's that?" Papa looked as if he'd been struck in the face with what Ben had told him.

"I was saying I didn't dive, sir. I mean I was more careful. I know to be careful," Ben said.

"Let's don't be nickel and diming the rules here, young man. What I say in this family is not something you can carve away at, not something you can shape to be the way you want it to be when you want it to be different." Papa moved his face in front of Ben's to force him to look right at him.

"All I can say," Papa went on, "is it's a good thing your Mama won't ever know—" Then his shoulders sagged like something that held him together on the inside had come apart. "I'm sorry," he said. "Saying that about your mama isn't fair." He shook his head. "It's just that you kids are all I've got now," and he put an arm around Ben's shoulders and began to walk him toward the barn. "You're all I've got anymore." His face looked like old rags just then. "Sometimes I get just plain scared."

"Yes, sir."

"What d'you say we put this behind us then." Papa said. "I expect you know you've done wrong."

Ben grunted and looked ashamed.

I didn't like thinking that my papa would ever be scared by anything. I picked up the cat and held her to where I could make her look me in the face. "Don't you ever go to the quarry, Clementine," I said. "You hear me? You just stay in the barn and watch for rats, and we'll be okay."

By the time Ben had set the milk out in pans to cool, Ingrid had supper on the table. It happened to be pot roast with dumplings, Ben's favorite, but he didn't say a word except please and thank you all through the meal. The clock seemed to tick louder than usual.

I knew that the wager between Jake and Papa had been settled while we were at school that day. But the fun of their silly bet had been stolen by the hard feelings of Ben disobeying and Papa being disappointed in him. Jake might not have known the particulars, but

he must have sensed something in the air. He didn't
say anything. He's not the sort to interfere with family
matters. By the time we finished Ingrid's rice pudding
with jam on the top, I was glad supper was over and we
didn't all have to sit there brooding anymore. Without
having to be asked, I cleared the table and began washing the dishes.

With supper over, Papa and Ben wandered off some
place. I think Papa wanted to take advantage of Ben's
sheepishness and get him to do some extra chore,
maybe tinker with our tractor, which had been acting
up. Ingrid had reading to do for school. That left Jake
and me.

"Well, Katy Sue," he said, as he dried the last plate
and put it on the shelf. "I need an assistant and it looks
as if you're elected." He spread a linen cloth on the
kitchen table and set up his bird things. "Your papa got
one crow this morning, and I got the other. I can't say
who was first 'cause we went out in separate directions.
And I won't say which is which either; they look about
the same at this point anyway. Gonna skin 'em both."

Jake untied the cord on a cloth pouch and unrolled
a row of pockets that held special tiny scissors and

every kind of long tweezers and tiny knives that he called scalpels. "Be a good girl and go down to the cellar, won't you, and bring up the victims. You'll find our two specimens wrapped in paper down there where it's cool. Don't touch the feathers, 'case they have any bugs in 'em."

Our kitchen has a door into the parlor and another that goes down the hall to the bathroom, which Papa says was added on. Before we dug the new well, the bathroom that went with our house was on the outside. On the other side of the kitchen is our back porch, which is screened in. You can lift a hatch in the floor back there and go down the stairs to the cellar. Everything we put up from the garden goes below the house: jams and pickles, jars of corn and beans and applesauce, and anything else we might be wanting to perk up a winter meal. Jake had put the crows down there to keep them fresh.

You can't tell the true size of a crow when it perches on a fence off in the distance. In my hands, those birds felt almost as heavy and big as bantam chickens. I took care to leave them in their rolled-up newspapers as Jake had told me. You wouldn't think a common crow would ever feel like a treasure, but I walked back into the kitchen as if I were carrying a fancy glass pitcher of lemonade that I didn't want to spill.

I had never liked crows. Their voices sounded like metal to me, and I thought they moved around as if they were always looking to pick a fight. Seeing those two up close, though, with their featherless gray eyelids closed, I felt sorry for them. On a farm, we see a lot of dead animals. We don't have time to feel sorry for every single one. Still, I wondered if the crows' families knew that they'd been shot.

Jake told me that crows are very social animals and aren't stupid like chickens. They're intelligent enough to have a sort of language among themselves. He said crows will hide things and remember where they've put them.

"Chickens would never do that," I said.

"No. And chickens don't have a sense of family, either. Crows keep track of who is who. Maybe they can do that because they don't raise as many chicks at a time—usually only three," Jake said, and I thought, *That's how many our mama had.*

I looked at the two black birds with new respect. Jake took them from me like an expert. By then he had his little bottles set up. One was labeled in brown handwriting. It said *Arsenic*. Underneath was a skull and crossbones. No one had to tell me not to touch it.

Jake cut with his scissors and then pulled the skin away, just like when Papa slaughtered a bull calf, only the crow was more delicate. "The trick is to leave the fascia—this inner skin—intact and not break into the body cavity," he said.

"You mean the guts?" I asked. "Would you ever put a crow in your museum?"

"I think I might."

"Would city kids know what a crow sounded like?" I asked. I thought about their hoarse caws and how they interrupt each other rudely.

"City kids see crows at garbage dumps. They make plenty of racket there."

"Are you going to stuff Papa's crow?"

"You'll see," Jake said. He crunched through some of the thin bones with his instruments. He left the feet connected to the skins and he left the wing tips and the beaks, but he took away the eyeballs. When he had everything separated, Jake set aside the naked flesh of both crows in a fold of newspaper. Next, he powdered the insides of the skins with something from a little jar.

"What's that?" I asked.

"Cornmeal. That's to dry 'em out," he said. Next, he pulled a piece off a roll of cotton batting that came wound around crinkly blue paper. He wadded up the cotton into a ball and picked it up with his tweezers. He scooted the arsenic bottle away from where I was sitting, a bottle maybe twice the size of his thumb, and removed its ground-glass stopper, taking care not to touch the inside part of the stopper. He dipped the ball of cotton into the white powder. "This'll discourage any bugs that might want to have bird skin for their suppers," he said, as he dabbed the poison all around and on top of where the cornmeal had stuck.

Next, he made four smaller balls of cotton and poked them in where the birds' eyes had been. "We'll get 'em some proper glass eyes at the museum," he said, "but this'll hold 'em for now." The crows looked spooky with nothing but white showing in their eye holes. He took a length of black silk thread off a wooden spool and found the opening of a curved needle that he took out of a red felt holder. Using another kind of tweezers that had handles like scissors, he stitched closed the belly cuts he'd made. With the extra thread he tied each pair of skritchy feet and stretched them out toward the tail. He folded the wings flat along the bodies and smoothed all the feathers down.

Last, Jake took two little white tags out of a brown envelope. Each had a hole through the edge and a string in the hole. He wrote the date and his initials on both of them and tied one to each crow at the feet. "When we get 'em to the museum, we'll mount 'em so they look lifelike," he said. He tied up his tweezers and the rest of his kit. "And I guarantee you," he said, "no matter how torn up your daddy is over losing your mama, Charles Hanson is going to have one big belly laugh the day these crows fly again." He winked. I didn't know what he meant by that, but I knew he had something playful up his sleeve.

"But for now, little Katydid," Jake said, "this show is over. And I thank you for your help."

He knew and I knew that all I had done was watch.

EIGHT

I never did get around to asking Jake to help me with my drawing for Mrs. Breton. Two days later, when Ingrid and I came home from school, he was gone. Papa said Jake's cranes were finally ready to have their photographs taken and that Jake had asked Papa to say his good-byes. On the kitchen table Jake had left a roll of film. It was out of what he called his people camera, and on it there were pictures of all of us. All Papa had to do was take the film to the pharmacy and get it developed.

Upstairs on my pillow Jake had left his little box of water paints, with a note saying he'd get himself a new set. I thought of making Mrs. Breton a picture of our family instead of the crows, and this time I'd remember to put myself in it. But school was almost out. I decided she'd probably forgotten about my drawing pictures anyway.

With Jake gone, the house sounded hollow and felt gray again. Every shuffle and cough rattled around the walls like little stones. Jake had made us laugh. During the few days he spent with us, his company had made us forget what had happened to us. Still, in the quiet of it being just us Hansons, I felt more myself. We could be crabby with each other if we needed to be and not worry about being polite for an outsider.

⟨❧⟩

That Saturday Ingrid didn't get out of bed in the morning.

"Are you sick?" I asked, as I stood between our two beds in my nightie.

"Not exactly. I think I got my first monthly," she said.

"You *did*? In the night? What's it feel like, anyway?" I knew about getting the monthlies and how it was like the cows when they're ready to mother a calf. There's no farm kid who doesn't know about things like that.

"Awful." She moaned and turned toward the window and onto her side, rolling up into a ball.

"You gotta tell Papa, then."

"Are you joking? I can't do that," she said. "If it were a school day, I could go to the nurse."

"Ingrid," I said, "you should tell Papa."

"You tell him if you think he should know so darned much."

I went only as far as our bedroom door, not knowing

whether to go back in and talk to my sister or run and get help. I didn't know what to do. It was plain, though, that Ingrid wasn't going to take care of her own needs.

Papa and Ben were already out in the barn. It was a sure thing I didn't want Ben to hear. He'd have just hooted and teased.

I went out into the yard with bare feet and still dressed in my nightie. Dew was damp on the grass and the air rose up warm from morning's long, clean shadows.

Papa was sitting on the stool milking Daphne. Ben had finished up with Emeline. I leaned my head against Daphne's big tan flank. "Papa," I whisper-shouted to get his attention over the *tshh-tshh-tshh* of the milk hitting the pail.

"Hang on there, Katy Sue. Can't you see I'm working?"

"But, Papa, it's about Ingrid." He looked up, his hands still holding Daphne's teats but his squeezing rhythm interrupted. Daphne stomped one foot impatiently.

"It's—it's—," I said, "well, I can't say right now, but it's something important about Ingrid."

Papa called to Ben, "Finish up with Daphne here, would you? I'll be right back."

"You should get something on your feet, Katy Sue,"

Papa said, "It's not summer yet." We blinked under the sudden sunlight after being inside the barn. "Now, what's all this about Ingrid?"

Something unexpected tied my tongue into knots.

"She's not sick, is she?" I knew Papa kept a close eye on my sister, being as how she was the most susceptible to getting melancholy from time to time. "Or is she crying again? Is that it?"

"No. She's, uh—" Then I blurted out, "Ingrid's got her first monthly."

His face lit up like a celebration. "So that's it. Well, we should tell your ma—" Right away he caught himself and said more quietly, "So that's it," and then to himself, "I see."

He squatted down so he could look right into my face. "I expect Ingrid'll need some fixings, won't she? You go into your mama's closet and way in the back you'll find what Ingrid needs. You take that to her and tell her if it's not right we'll get her whatever else she needs in town this afternoon." Then he added, "This means Ingrid's a grown-up girl, you know."

"Papa," I said, looking down at my bare toes in the gravel of our lane, "don't tell Ben, okay?"

"No. There are some things that boys just don't understand. Even nice boys like Ben."

Later on that day Aunt Rosa and Uncle Dennis

came for a visit and Aunt Rosa went off with Ingrid. I don't know what they said exactly, but I think Aunt Rosa was trying to take Mama's place. For a minute I almost hated her for that.

With family visiting, we all went to the linden tree to sit on the grass for a spell. Papa said a prayer and we stood up and held hands in a big circle. I was between Ben and Uncle Dennis. My uncle's hands are so big that he squished my finger bones together, and he didn't even know it.

The afternoon was closing up and it looked like rain. It was time for our relatives to go back to their own place. I heard Papa and them talking. Aunt Rosa's high-up voice was the only one I could make out. "It's one thing with Ben," she said, "he's almost a man and near ready to be on his own soon enough." What Uncle Dennis and Papa said was rumbly and low. "Charles, you *can't* raise those two girls by yourself," my aunt interrupted. She's Papa's sister by marriage and doesn't always know our family's ways. "You've *got* to think about getting—" and that's all I could hear before Uncle Dennis gunned the engine. I didn't know why she sounded so stern with my papa, but I trusted him to stand up to whatever it was that had her wound so tight.

That night Papa was real quiet but sort of edgy. Finally, he said he needed privacy to make a call. Our telephone is on the wall between the kitchen and the parlor. Naturally, I was curious, so on my way upstairs, I dawdled long enough to hear what he said to the operator. He asked her to ring Aunt Katherine's number.

I could hear through the floor that they talked a long time. Considering it was a toll call to Chesterton, I would have expected him to wrap things up quicker.

A few days later, Ingrid and I got off the school bus and checked our mailbox, as we often did. It stood on a timber at the county road. We were thinking there might be a postcard from Jake. Instead we saw a letter with our aunt's handwriting. It was all alone in the mailbox, a crisp blue envelope addressed to Papa. Ingrid put the letter inside the front cover of her social studies book, and we found Papa in the garden watering the bean plants. We waited while he read it, but he didn't tell us what it said. He just wiped his chin back and forth with one hand while he read the letter again. He studied the sky for a good long while, as if the clouds might hold the answer to a question we didn't know about. Then he went back to his beans. You'd think he hadn't even noticed that Ingrid and I had been standing there the whole time, wanting to hear whatever the news was.

At supper Papa finally said, "What would you kids think of having your Aunt Katherine come to stay? Permanently, I mean."

So that was it. I looked to Ingrid to see whether it was a good idea or not.

"She *was* your mama's sister," Papa went on, "so it's not like we'd be having a stranger in the house. Ingrid, it'd lighten your load."

"It surely would, sir," she said, but she answered too quickly and then stared off into space. I couldn't tell whether she really accepted the idea.

"Ben?"

"What about her school teaching and all?" he asked.

"She's prepared to give that up for the sake of you kids here. But, hey, let's don't rush into anything. We can let it ride for a time. Whatever happens, you kids come first."

I shouldn't have been surprised that Ingrid didn't give an honest answer. She'd always been one to say any old thing and then drift away inside herself, sitting in the rocking chair and staring at nothing. But since Mama died, Ingrid had gotten worse.

Sometimes she'd hold her doll with the porcelain

face. That night she took her horse figurine down from the shelf. Mama had given her that china horse, so it had special meaning. She held it and stroked it and held it and stroked it, tears running down all the while and her not taking the trouble to wipe them off. She stared straight ahead at nothing, at some secret in the air that none of us could see.

"Ingrid?" I said, but she didn't move. She seemed to be far away from us. We didn't know how to find her when she got like that. It seemed as though we might burn her skin with our fingers if we tried to touch her.

The next day Ingrid barely had what it took to care for herself, let alone help anyone else with their needs. Papa did my braids, but they turned out crooked. Mrs. Breton took pity on me at school and combed them out and fixed them again with new rubber bands from her desk. She folded the ends back onto themselves, and the tips of my braids poked my neck all the rest of that day.

Dr. Hamilton came out to the house at suppertime. He talked to Ingrid low and soft in the parlor. I peeked in from the kitchen but couldn't hear what they were saying, and Ben shooed me off anyway. I don't think she looked up at the doctor's face one single time.

Later, on the porch, Dr. Hamilton said, "There's no disease in Ingrid. What she needs isn't medicine."

"You can't do anything for her?" Papa asked. He tried to give the doctor a five dollar bill for coming out, but the doctor wouldn't take it.

"No, unfortunately I can't do a thing, Charles." Dr. Hamilton laid his hand on Papa's shoulder and looked him square in the face. "But you can. You all can," he looked to Ben and me. "What Ingrid needs is whatever love you can muster." Ben shifted his weight and Papa put his arm around my shoulders and drew me close to his side. "Just love her as much as you can and allow her to be the way she needs to be right now," the doctor went on, "and don't lean on her to snap out of it. This'll take time, with Edna gone and all that." He started for his car, then turned back and shifted his black leather bag from one hand to the other, "I was thinking," he called gently across the early evening, "is there some relative or someone you have who could come help out?" He paused and waved his hand through the air as if he could erase what he'd just said. "Never mind. It's not my place to butt in. I'm just so terribly sorry." He shook his head slowly from side to side and drove off.

That night Papa again asked the operator to get Aunt Katherine on the telephone. We'd been expecting her to come for a summer visit and then return to her teaching in August. But she and Papa must have come to a new understanding, because later I learned that's when she handed in her resignation to the school board and made plans to come and stay with us for good.

NINE

On the last day of school I told Mrs. Breton that I'd miss her over the summer.

"Don't forget to draw whatever beauty you see in the world, Katy Sue," she said. She straightened my collar. "There's no such thing as too much art."

So, she hadn't forgotten. I promised myself I'd get out Jake's watercolors and make her a picture after all. But it wouldn't be of Mama and it wouldn't be of crows. Pictures like that were too hard for me.

Papa fetched Aunt Katherine in our truck. It was the middle of June, three months since Mama had died. Papa and Ben had already cut the first hay, and it hurt to walk barefoot on the stubble.

Papa moved himself to the spare bedroom downstairs and left the big room upstairs for Aunt Katherine. Maybe he felt guilty that she would have to do all the inside work, even though we weren't meant to be her responsibility.

For sisters, I wouldn't say that my aunt and my
mother looked alike. Mama had wavy dark hair, but
Aunt Katherine's was more straight, and brown like raw
sugar. She wore bangs but combed them to the side,
and if it was windy she tied it all under a kerchief. Aunt
Katherine was tall and thin. Some of her bones showed
through, and she had a way of standing or sitting like
a model in the *Woman's Home Companion*. She could
have been a movie star. Mama didn't wear lipstick, but
Aunt Katherine did—Fire Engine Red, by Tangee.

Aunt Katherine brought her own kitchenware and
special gadgets that she liked, a thing for opening tight
jar lids and a potato masher with a green handle that
she said had been our grandmother's. She brought a
trunk of clothes and a hat with real fur around the
edge. She brought framed pictures of herself and Mama
with their brothers, my uncles, when they were little.
She brought books and her own shelf to put them on.
Some of the books were children's stories, and I was
allowed to read them if I asked permission first and
remembered to say please and thank you. She brought
a rocking chair that matched our grandmother's blue
furniture in the parlor, and she put hers alongside ours.
While she was in there she lifted the window shades.
"It's more important to have fresh air and light than to
worry about whether the sun will fade some rug that

you hardly ever walk on anyway," she said. It felt good to have someone take over, and not to be tip-toeing around anymore.

At the same time I felt guilty for being glad to have Aunt Katherine come live with us. I knew she wasn't trying to take over Mama's place the way Aunt Rosa had. Aunt Katherine had never been that kind of person.

*

The morning after Aunt Katherine arrived, Ben came into the kitchen and jerked his head toward the stairs as if I should follow him. Ingrid was already up in our room. The three of us went into a huddle.

"Now, the way I see it," Ben began. He was trying to sound like a big shot, as if he was in charge of the three of us all of a sudden. "We're going to have to pull together with Aunt Katherine here and all."

Ingrid said, "It's not as if she's never visited before, you know."

"Right," said Ben, "but I'm thinking there's going to be a period of adjustment. Like when folks get a new truck and you know not to drive it too fast till the engine's broken in. She's not just visiting this time."

"Yeah, Ingrid," I said. "Aunt Katherine's here *forever*." She gave me a look.

"See, this is what I mean," said Ben. He looked from Ingrid to me and back again, exasperated with us. "We have to be on our very best behavior."

"For Aunt Katherine?" said Ingrid, "like she's a saint or something?"

"No," Ben said, "for Papa. He's the one caught in the middle here. I mean, sure, Aunt Katherine's going to help out and all, but Papa and her might not exactly be best friends, you know. The last thing he needs is any of us squabbling or talking back."

I asked, "D'you think if we like Aunt Katherine being here it means we don't still miss Mama?"

Ingrid rolled her eyes.

Ben put one hand on my shoulder. He said, "Having her here will probably make you miss Mama even more."

"Because she's different from Mama?" I asked.

"Because she's so much the same," he said. "And," he added, "because she's gentle and because she loves us."

Ingrid said, "She'll never love us the way Mama did."

"So what?" I said, and gave Ingrid back the mean look she'd given me. "No one's ever going to do that."

"Just let's all be on good behavior," Ben said. I felt good about my brother looking out for our family, but I felt mean toward Ingrid for not cooperating.

Papa asked the blessing that first night when all five of us sat down at the kitchen table. "Dear Lord," he said quietly, "we are much obliged to you for sending Katherine to us. We are thankful for her devotion to this family. Bless her and bless the memory of her sister." Then, as an afterthought, he added, "And bless this food which we are about to receive. Amen."

At first I didn't know how I felt about having Aunt Katherine with us. I didn't know whether it was disloyal to Mama's memory for me to accept her as part of our permanent family, or disloyal to my brother for not accepting her. It had always been fun when she'd come for a visit. She and Mama would be in each other's pockets, singing and dancing around if a Hoagy Carmichael song came on the radio.

To have my aunt with us forever, though, and maybe telling us how to behave or ordering us around was sort of scary. All of a sudden I realized I didn't know her ways. I was afraid I might do things that would make her angry. Also, she and Papa seemed to have some grit between them about how strict to be with the rules. That made me nervous.

On the other hand, Ingrid's outlook picked up, and that surprised me. Although Ingrid liked to complain about having to do the kitchen work, she let everyone know in no uncertain terms that the cooking was her territory and hers alone, and for me not to butt in with my opinions on how things should be done, or even help her figure out what to cook. When Aunt Katherine arrived, Ingrid must have been ready to share the job. Maybe it worked out because our aunt started by asking Ingrid how she'd like things done and by taking on the cleanup, which Ingrid hated anyway. Also, having help with the work gave Ingrid more time to read her books. My sister had always been one to disappear into a story whenever she got the chance.

Aunt Katherine was cheerful to us kids. She didn't hog the bathroom as Ben had feared she would. She found things to like about farm life and asked us how this or that thing worked, or where we liked the broom kept, or if we minded having the radio on a certain music station. She liked that the eggs were warm when I brought them in from the nests, and that we had all the thick yellow cream a family could ever want after the milk settled in its pans. She didn't mind that Ben would come in from chores and chin himself on the doorway.

Aunt Katherine could do things that seemed special. She could whistle the same lacy twist of notes that the wood thrushes sang in the pasture, and she knew the names of all the moon cycles, like the Planter's Moon and the Wolf Moon. She could fry doughnuts so they came out crisp on the outside and soft in the middle, and they didn't taste greasy after they cooled. She picked daisies and cornflowers along the ditch and put them in a vinegar bottle, with red columbine that she found in the woods. And while she was at the edge of our woods she saw that the wild strawberries were ripe. Everyone knows the wild ones are best.

She called out to Ingrid and me and gave us each a little basket to hold what we picked. She said the berries would give our cream a purpose and she walked Ingrid and me back to where they grew. Each of us ate so many, though, right then and there, that we didn't have enough to fill a single bowl, so we sat down on last year's leaves and ate the rest, one by one, taking turns.

Finally, Aunt Katherine pulled the hull off the juiciest, fattest, reddest berry and held it out toward Ingrid. She said, "Here's the best for last. Close your eyes and put this in your mouth, and see whether you don't hear the angels singing."

Ingrid popped the berry into her mouth and licked around her lips, like a cat lapping. "I hear them. I hear them," she said, still with her eyes closed, and I knew one of those singing angels was my mama. That's how sweet the berries were.

Aunt Katherine had a nice way about her when it came to appreciating treats. On the Fourth of July she was up with the sun, early and bright. She busied herself with picnic fixings while Ben and Papa were pulling up the straps to their overalls and making their way through the kitchen and out to the barn. I sat at the table in my nightclothes, still waking up.

Daphne and Emeline had to get milked as usual; they don't understand holidays. And the pigs needed their slops. I dressed myself and gave the chickens their corn and gathered all the eggs. Ingrid turned the calves out into their pasture.

After morning chores, though, it wasn't a day for working.

Aunt Katherine made a breakfast of buttermilk pancakes and slabs of ham. Ingrid opened the last jar of applesauce. I tidied up the dishes without being asked, and Ingrid started peeling the potatoes for salad. She saw that Aunt Katherine had set a jar of sweet pickles alongside the big blue bowl.

"Couldn't we make it the way Mama always did?" Ingrid asked. "Mama was famous, you know, for stirring up the best potato salad."

"I'm counting on you knowing how," my aunt said.

"It's just that Mama never used sweet pickles," Ingrid said. "She swore by dills."

"Is that a fact? Your grandma always used sweet."

"Papa prefers it with dill."

"Oh." Aunt Katherine's mouth pinched up as if she was all of a sudden smelling something bad. "You girls have a lot of special requests, don't you?"

My face burned hot at how quickly she turned on us.

"Well, fine," she said. But things in the room had shifted. "Katy Sue, go on down to the cellar then and bring up whatever this family considers the proper pickles for potatoes."

I tried to make a joke, "That sounds like a tongue twister."

Ingrid caught my eye and then turned to Aunt Katherine and made a little laugh that came out more like a cough. "She sells seashells . . . ," she began.

Aunt Katherine picked up a wooden spoon and waved it like an orchestra director, as if nothing had happened. "Peter Piper picked a peck of pickled—uh, potatoes?" She smiled.

I guess I smiled, too, on my way to the cellar, but I was learning that we had to be careful.

Ingrid made an applesauce cake with what remained of the quart she'd opened. Papa walked through the kitchen and dragged his finger through the batter. He tasted it and said it needed more cinnamon. Ingrid scolded him for licking, but you could tell she was kidding. After he went out, she added another shake or two of spices.

There was more ham to slice for sandwiches and mustard to spread on the bread and young carrots from the garden to cut up for eating raw. I took the feathery tops to the chickens, because Ben said carrot tops make the egg yolks richer and more yellow. Ingrid put a butter frosting on her cake and that went into its own basket. Papa mixed the lemonade and washed a million radishes to go with the carrots. The radish leaves also went to the chickens.

"What about my pigs?" Ben asked with a pretend whine. "They don't get any treats for Independence Day? How come it's always Katy Sue's chickens that're first in line for greens?"

"Here," said Aunt Katherine. "Some lovely eggshells and two burned pancakes." She looked around the kitchen. "Oh, and these delicious lemon rinds." She added them to the enamel slop pail that we use.

"Pigs won't eat citrus," Ben said. "It's about the only thing they'll turn up their snouts at. But I'll take these potato parings." Ben was always looking out for the pigs, because he wanted to enter them in the county fair that year.

Papa drove us all to Lake Augusta in the truck. Half the town was there. Ingrid went off with Emily Brownfield. Janice Huntington had to mind her little sister, so they came over and sat on our blanket.

I had never seen Aunt Katherine in a swimsuit before. She wore a two-piece like ladies in the magazines, and the skin between her shorts and top was pale as winter butter. She was younger than Mama and didn't have any blue veins in her legs.

Lots of people came by to introduce themselves and make it clear that they had known my mama. You could tell that some of them thought it was nice that Aunt Katherine had come to stay, but others were going to wait and see, which I thought was mean of them. Who were they to judge what our family ought to do?

Papa took me swimming in the lake. He said he'd be my lifeguard in case I had a mind to go under, but I'm a good swimmer. He showed me how to hold my breath and stand on my hands under water and wag my feet in the air. Then he let me ride on his back while he stroked us out to the floating dock.

By late afternoon we were ready to go into town and find ourselves a place on the grass for watching the fireworks later. At the city park there were men selling hot dogs and watermelon and taffy. Papa said we weren't required to eat a balanced meal and gave us each half a dollar to spend any way we wanted. Mama would never have done that. She'd have known I'd get a tummy ache.

Up until the Fourth of July it seemed as if Aunt Katherine liked me most of the time. Some days it was like a party having her with us in our house. After a while, though, she started correcting me and finding fault here and there, like if I didn't sit up straight enough at the dinner table, or telling me I shouldn't pick at a scab on my leg even if it itched. It began to rub me raw having her there morning, noon, and night. I didn't want her to think I was tiresome or stupid. I always tried to be on my best behavior.

One afternoon I picked her some nasturtiums. Those golden flowers had gone wild where Mama had had her window garden. I was hoping I could make my aunt notice me.

"I had a hunch you like flowers," I said. Aunt Katherine was sitting by the window mending socks.

"Oh, I do. I do. But, Katy Sue, look here." She pointed to the stems. "These are covered all over with aphids."

Sure enough, those bugs, smaller than pinheads, were lined up along each wiry stem. I didn't think any of them would come off if we put the flowers right 'quick into a bottle. Aphids are sticky. I wiped my hands down my skirt. Maybe a couple were on me from the picking, but I didn't mind if they were. They barely showed on the nasturtiums anyway, being as how they were the same light green as the stems. Only a finicky person would have inspected that close.

"Better take them back outside." Aunt Katherine handed me the bouquet.

I threw them on the ground behind the henhouse and stomped them with my shoe. Then, remembering how much hens like to eat bugs, I was sorry I hadn't fed them to the chickens.

The next day I took Aunt Katherine marigolds, but she said marigolds were to be enjoyed outside and that they'd stink up the kitchen with their funny odor. After that I didn't take her any flowers for a long time.

Another time I put our calico cat in her lap, thinking she might like the feel of Clementine's soft fur, but Aunt Katherine leapt up like I'd put a cowpie on her or something. She said cats made her sneeze. I didn't know she had any allergy. I felt as if I always had to worry about making mistakes around her.

Finally, I came right out and said, "Well, I just guess I can't do anything right, can I?"

She said, "We all need to learn to relax around each other. Maybe you're trying too hard to be perfect. Perfection is a strain on anybody."

"But I'm afraid if I make too many mistakes you won't like me," I said, trying not to cry.

"I like you just fine the way you are, Katy Sue."

I didn't believe her about liking me. I didn't see how she could if she had to keep correcting me. The old Aunt Katherine who'd been so much fun when Mama was alive began to seem uncommonly picky.

※

By the time our raspberries grew red and heavy, I didn't think Aunt Katherine was pretty anymore. Of course, I kept that to myself.

The weather had grown hot with summer. It wasn't enough that I had to put all the berries into their little wooden boxes pointing the same way. She suggested, too, that I'd want to be careful not to bruise any, or that this one might have been too green to pick, or that one might have been overripe.

Half our crop went to Papa, who sold the best berries

in town. The other half was for us, and those I didn't
have to arrange any special way.

Ingrid knew how to make jam, and because Aunt
Katherine had never learned to put food by before
she came to our house, it was Ingrid who stood at the
stove. I fought the sun and the stickers, while Ingrid
dealt with the heat of the kitchen. Steam and sweat
stuck wisps of hair to her face, but I was hot all over
my skin. I had to move an empty crate along the rows
and climb up on it to be tall enough to reach the
prickly canes of the berry bushes.

Aunt Katherine's excuse for never cooking jam
herself was that her school kids had always brought her
plenty. Oh, she'd say, there'd be the boy who came in
with a pint of apple butter or the girl whose mother
made the best watermelon pickles you ever tasted.
She had a habit of running her hand along her neck
in a way that made me think she felt more important
than the rest of us. Her stories made that classroom of
hers sound like a regular old general store, with those
goody-goody students who brought in their bushels of
pears in the fall or sacks of rhubarb in the spring and
gave her tins of pulled mints at Christmastime.

"What about when you were little?" Ingrid asked.
"Who cooked the preserves when you and Mama

were girls?" Ingrid ladled the foam out of her bubbling pot and put it into a pie tin. I hoped we'd be allowed to spread that sweet pink froth on slices of bread when it cooled.

"Well, our mama did," Aunt Katherine said, "your grandma. But she was always too busy to show us how and then I was off to get my teaching credentials." She pointed to the tiniest splot on the linoleum, maybe one teeny little raspberry seed and one speck of juice. "Katy Sue, there's a berry on the floor. Would you mind?"

Ingrid said, "I'm sure she didn't mean to step on it."

Aunt Katherine answered, "I'm not saying she did. It's just that someone needs to clean it up, that's all."

I took the dish rag from the sink and started toward the splot.

"Let's not use the dish rag, Katy Sue," Aunt Katherine said. "What you use on the plates is not what you ought to wipe the floor with. I'll get the string mop." Then she started banging around the back porch with the galvanized metal bucket, and I went back to the field.

I picked berries every day that week and into the next. Then we had a day of rain, which we needed, because our soil was dry and cracking, but you can't pick raspberries in the rain, else they'll rot on you. Despite all the rain, the weather didn't cool.

At lunchtime everyone talked about the heat. Ben said, "Think about a time in winter when you felt too cold. Then you won't feel so sticky and hot right now." He stood up, forgetting to push in his chair, and stuffed another muffin in his mouth on the way out the door. But Ben could do no wrong in Aunt Katherine's eyes. It was always, Ben, could you reach me this or that on the high shelf? or, Oh, it must be nice to be so tall, or, Ben, dear, could you just help with this lid? Then she'd hand him a bottle whose cap was screwed on too tight for her hands, which were big compared to mine but scrawny and bony looking like hen's feet.

Ingrid was Little Miss Perfect. It seemed as if she was never scolded and never corrected for her grammar. But then Ingrid rarely made mistakes.

On an afternoon hot enough to melt the tongue right out of your mouth, I was trying to follow Ben's advice. "Aunt Katherine?" I said, "did you ever hear about the time we got stuck in a snowbank?"

"No, I don't believe I have."

"Well, it was Feb'uary. Papa got the truck stuck so bad we couldn't get to church and we couldn't get home and Mr. Culshank had to help us with his tractor and then he got stuck and we all helped him out and that was that."

My aunt said, "There are two R's in February, Katy Sue."

"I know. But you see, we had to all get into the snowbank, and the wind was howling—Mama, too—and we pushed an—"

"Feb-*rew*-ary," Aunt Katherine said.

Ingrid was listening. "But you could tell what she meant," she said, sticking up for me.

"And Katy Sue, please don't drag your feet when you walk. You'll scuff your shoes," said Aunt Katherine.

Ingrid stuck up for me again, "But that's the way Katy Sue has always walked." I couldn't stop the hot tears from dribbling down my cheeks.

"Well, I guess I can't do *anything* that pleases you, can I?" I shouted. I ran out the door and let the screen slap and bang on its jamb any old way. Then I banged it again on purpose to make sure everyone knew the first time wasn't any accident. I didn't care what Aunt Katherine thought. I even wished it had banged louder.

"C'mon Clementine," I said, and took up the cat. We huffed through the orchard and past the well. "We're not ever going back in there no matter what. Never, never, never, are we?" I asked.

We crossed the grassy draw and up the hill to Mama's

grave. I hugged that soft kitty up to me tight. She let me wipe my tears in her fur, even though she was probably scared out of her wits and couldn't breathe with me clutching her like that. Finally, I leaned up against the big trunk of the linden tree, letting her loose into my lap, and cried and cried and cried.

I wanted everything to be different. I wanted everything to be the same as it used to be. I wanted my mama to come back, even if it was just long enough to put Aunt Katherine in her place.

Eventually, I saw Papa heading up the hill. Ingrid must have fetched him. Or maybe Aunt Katherine. He sat and took the cat from me and set her aside, then he gathered me up in his arms. His blue shirt smelled of him and of the cows and of the fields and of the sun.

He waited a good long while before he said, "You're going to have to build yourself up to where you can make an apology, you know."

"I'm not sorry," I said. "I hate her, Papa. I hate that mean old Aunt Katherine."

"Now *hate* is a mighty strong word, little one. I expect you are talking out of anger and frustration more than hate. Don't you suppose that might be?" He lifted my chin with one finger and looked into my face. "You are a sight, little Katydid. I swear." He smoothed my hair and braids and cleaned up my face as best he could with his big kerchief. At least he didn't make me lick it first. And he didn't lick it for me, which would have been worse. He covered my nose with the cloth and said when to blow, like when I was a little girl. It felt good to have him care for me, but I wasn't finished sulking.

I said, "Sometimes it seems as if Aunt Katherine is trying to be our mama."

"Maybe she is, maybe she isn't. We can't control other people's behavior, can we?"

"But she's *not* our mama."

"Each of us is responsible for our own actions. It's not our place to judge the actions of others. All's I know is that your mama would be happy to know that her sister gave up her life in Chesterton to be with us here, and that's what matters. Aunt Katherine is a hard worker. She's a kind and decent woman. She deserves our thanks and our respect."

"But she's mean to me."

"See if you can't give her another chance, little Katydid." He looked at me. "Now let's take you in and get you put back together, shall we? I have something inside to show you, anyway."

I think what made me want to go along with him is that Papa didn't rush me or yank on me to get me down to the house. He let me take my time along the way. We went in at the front door and into the parlor, where he said to sit myself in the big rocker and he'd be right back. He brought my brush and comb from upstairs and a wet facecloth from the bathroom. He wiped my cheeks and fixed my hair as best he could. My braids were crooked like always when he took charge of them, but it didn't matter.

Next, he put himself in the rocker and drew me onto his lap, my legs dangling over the edge of him.

"You've spent a lot of time with Aunt Katherine in this chair, you know."

"I have?"

"Why, when you were just a whiff of a tiny baby and your mama was all tuckered out from birthing you, you got the colic."

"I did?"

"Well, it's natural that your mama wanted her sister here to help out with things, seeing as how their mama was gone by then, God rest her soul. She had Ingrid and Ben to tend to and they were little, and I had the farm to work and the winter wood to get in and the crops to put by."

"What happened?" I said.

"Well, seemed like nothing would soothe you except getting rocked back and forth in this very chair. Back and forth. Back and forth, until you could let go of that tummy ache of yours and get yourself to sleep."

"Aunt Katherine did that?"

"She sat up most nights with you for the first weeks of your life, Katy Sue. After all, you were her namesake. She cared for you as much as any of us." He brushed my cheek with the back of his hand. "You don't want to be turning on her now. Besides, anger never does a body any good, anyway."

"But she's always picking on me."

"She'll learn more patience if we're patient with her. Nobody is perfect, Katy Sue. Nobody. She misses your mama just like we all do. We're all having a hard time with this. Remember, your Aunt Katherine knew Mama longer than any of us. They were sisters like you and Ingrid are. They had a life together for nineteen years before I ever set eyes on your mama."

"Mama was prettier than Aunt Katherine, wasn't she, Papa?"

"It's not fruitful to make comparisons, little Katydid. Not fruitful at all. Everyone is pretty in different ways, whether on the inside or on the out."

I settled into Papa's lap, curling up against his shirt. He rocked us slowly back and forth, while the sun found its way down the sky and behind the barn. I heard Ben with Daphne and Emeline, but Papa didn't stir. I felt that I could stay in his lap for as long as I needed to. That's when I remembered that he'd said he had something to show me.

By then, I didn't feel angry anymore anyway.

ELEVEN

*E*arlier that day Papa had stopped at the pharmacy to pick up the photographs from Jake's roll of film. The envelope of pictures was in the kitchen. So was Aunt Katherine.

"I'm sorry for slamming the door," I said.

"Well, sometimes in the hot weather people get on each other's nerves, don't they?" she said.

"I guess so," I said. Then I turned to go upstairs. On my way out of the kitchen I added, "not like in Feb'uary." But I said it under my breath so she and Papa couldn't hear me, and that made me feel better.

Papa had said we'd look at Jake's pictures after supper. As soon as we'd cleared everything off and washed the dishes, Papa spread the photographs out on the table. We passed them around and around. There were eleven of them, if you don't count the one that was crooked and showed only a patch of ground in it.

There was the one of Ben waving from the tractor, where the wind was lifting his hair up funny, and there was one of Ingrid feeding the calves. I liked the picture of Papa, Ben, Ingrid, and me standing in front of the house, although our faces were no bigger than butter beans, and the prints showed my pink pullover as being gray and our green shutters as black.

I wished there was one with Jake in it. It seemed funny to think back to when he'd been with us. His visit had been a happy time, even though Mama had already died. That was maybe the first time we'd all gotten away from our memories for a spell, even Ingrid.

"Aunt Katherine?" I said, not feeling cross with her anymore, "did you ever know our friend Jake? His real name is Mr. Jacobs."

"No, I don't believe I've ever met him."

"Well, he's nice," I said. "He took us for ice cream."

"Funny, too," Ingrid said.

"He's Papa's friend who works in the museum," said Ben. "The one I was telling you about."

I said, "Jake shot one of our crows when he was here. Look at this." I held out a picture of what Jake had called the two "victims" from the day of the wager. "Papa shot one, too, and Jake skinned them and took them to his museum. Jake says crows keep track of who their families are."

Aunt Katherine took the picture from me. Then she took up one that had the linden tree on the horizon.

Mama's marker was in the shadows, but you could see the hill and the tree. Jake must have stood in our orchard when he took that one. Then Aunt Katherine looked long and hard at a picture of all of us in front of the house. Everyone except her, that is. She looked at it for a good while. Maybe she took notice that we were all smiling that afternoon. Maybe she was trying to see Mama somewhere in the black and white of that shiny picture.

"Next time, you might be in the pictures with us, Aunt Katherine," I said, and looked toward Papa for approval. Having already said my formal apology, I wanted to make sure it stuck. Besides, Ingrid had told me I had to do more than just say I was sorry.

Later, when it was time to tuck me into bed, I said, "Aunt Katherine?"

"What is it?"

"I was angry with you earlier."

"Yes, I know. But you already apologized. And I'm sorry, too. If I was too critical, I mean."

"And Aunt Katherine?"

"Yes, dear."

I pulled my blanket up to my chin and snuggled my head into the pillow. "Do you think it's okay not to be sad every single day, even if our mama has died?"

She said, "Oh, absolutely. It's more than okay. Why,

it's your job. There's always good to be found in spite of a loss."

"That's funny," I said. "I thought tending the chickens was my job."

"Then you shall have two jobs." She smoothed my face with the flat of her hand. Her palm was soft and warm and smelled like some kind of flower. "Just as one of my jobs is to love you no matter what."

"Is that a hard job?" I asked. By then I had my covers up to my nose in case I had to hide from her answer.

"Not at all, little Katydid. It's the easiest thing in the world to do."

She turned out the light and paused at the door.

"Are you sad every day?" I asked.

She waited a minute with her hand on the doorknob the way Mama used to do. "I have my moments. I'll say that." Her head was down. "But it helps me to be here with you kids. I see your mama in you."

"In Ben and Ingrid, too?"

"In Ben and Ingrid, too." She blew me a kiss and left the door ajar for when Ingrid would come in later.

That was the first time Aunt Katherine had called me Katydid. I wasn't sure how I felt about her doing that. It was only my favorite people who used that name. I thought for a while, and then, just before I fell asleep, I decided it was all right.

That night I dreamed of Mama standing in Jake's picture of our hill. She had her arms full of butterflies. When I went close I saw light passing through her as if she were made of a dragonfly wing. The sun was behind her. It shone through her and made a dance of yellow dots on the backs of my hands when I looked down at myself. When I looked back up, Mama had turned into Aunt Katherine. She wore Mama's turquoise dress with the pin tucks around the yoke. The dots of light were on her hands, too, and yellow butterflies. Then Ingrid came up and touched my neck and said my name. Then I heard Ingrid really saying, "Katy Sue, Katy Sue, time to get up. We're having cinnamon toast for breakfast." And the sunlight was making patterns through the cherry tree outside our window.

At first, except for her gold wedding ring, we left Mama's belongings exactly where they'd always been. The ring went into a box on Papa's dresser, and he said, seeing as Ben was firstborn, it could be for Ben's wife if he ever found someone who would marry him. I was willing to bet he'd have hundreds to choose from, because Ben was nice looking and very polite. Most of the time.

Until Aunt Katherine came, Mama's clothes hung in her closet. Her silver hairbrush and hand mirror lay on her dresser. Then there was all that shuffling about, what with Papa taking the spare bedroom downstairs and leaving the big room for Aunt Katherine. Aunt Katherine packed Mama's belongings away under the eaves. She put them into the trunk she'd brought her own things in.

We were allowed to look in the trunk anytime we wanted. The turquoise dress from my dream was in there and Mama's other dresses and skirts and blouses and shoes and her blue coat with the shoulder pads and the hats she wore to Sunday services. We always kept mothballs with the woolens. The clothes had a sharp smell when I'd unfold them. Even so, I liked to get those things out and touch them, maybe even hold them up to me in front of the gold-framed mirror in Aunt Katherine's room. Mama had never let me play in her belongings the way some mothers will. I never dressed up in her high-heeled shoes or put her things on me for pretending. It would have felt wrong to put on anything from the trunk. Still, I could hold them up and look at myself in the mirror.

Papa put Mama's hairbrush and hand mirror in our room. "I expect you two will be wanting something of your Mama's," is what he said. We were meant to share, but he laid them on Ingrid's dresser, so they seemed more like hers than mine. She declared right away that we mustn't use them except on Sundays, and that I was to keep my hands off them in between and she would do the same. I wished they were mine alone. I didn't see the harm of looking in the mirror anytime I wanted. After all, it's not something that can wear out, and I wasn't about to be careless with it or let it get broken.

At least I could see the brush and mirror laid out there and think about how Mama looked when she primped or saw her reflection in that mirror. She would smooth her eyebrows into their arches or fluff her hair with one hand while she held the mirror up in front of her with the other. Then she'd check whether the back of her hair looked right. Her hair fell in just the right way, cut to shoulder length. She never had to pin it up at night or tie it in rags to get it to curl.

My hair is thicker than Ingrid's, but it's straight. That's why I have to wear it in braids. The little ends that don't get caught up in the pigtails are the only part with any curl. I asked Aunt Katherine if she'd cut bangs on me like how she wears hers, but she said maybe when I'm older. She has made French braids for me from time to time, with the French part running along either side of the top of my head. That keeps the wisps from getting loose.

The first time Papa saw me like that he pretended I was a stranger. "Who have we here?" he said. "A lovely young lady?" He bowed and kissed the back of my hand. "I am pleased to make the acquaintance of such an elegant miss." That made me laugh. I told him he was silly. Then he looked up at Aunt Katherine and smiled, and she smiled back in a slow, special way that lasted longer than I expected.

TWELVE

*B*y the end of July, Aunt Katherine and I had reached an understanding. It was all right for her to correct me from time to time—even my grammar—and she didn't mind me asking her occasionally whether she still loved me, just so I could make sure. She always said yes, that she still did love me and always would and for me not to worry about being a pest with my questions.

Of course, Mama was forever in my mind. Some things Aunt Katherine did were the same as how Mama had done them, but some things were different, like how she made up the beds with more top sheet folded over the blanket, or how she played the radio a little louder and a little more often. Papa said she'd wear it out if she wasn't careful, but he didn't make an issue of it as long as he could listen to the farm report in the morning. Once in a while when no one was around, I'd turn the dial to songs and dance around the kitchen to *Peg o' My Heart* or something by Guy Lombardo.

It was strange. I could be happy and dancing one minute and grieving the next. I couldn't tell when my sadness would hit. Once, during one of those songs on the radio, I just started crying. It never made any sense to me that I could be doing something I really liked, such as wading in the creek or sugaring strips of Aunt Katherine's excess pie crust to twist and bake alongside the pies, then next thing I knew I'd feel as sad as if Mama had just died yesterday. The sorrow would hit and spread inside me like warm water soaking into cloth.

With summer getting into August, the corn was high but not yet turned yellow. We were all anticipating the county fair. The year before, Mama had taken two blue ribbons and a red for her preserves. Now Ben wanted a ribbon for his pig. He started in to training it so when it came time to show it to the judges, the pig would know to mind him. After the judging, he was aiming to put his animal in the 4-H auction.

Papa has always said that he doesn't want to get into any hog breeding operations of our own, but he's happy to buy little ones from the Jessups' farm once they're weaned. After they reach ten pounds or so, piglets can be pulled off their mama and put onto slops or surplus milk from the cows or anything you happen to have. After that, a feeder pig's main job is to grow as big as it can as fast as it can. That's what

Ben says. We've never kept our own sow. We buy the piglets from Mr. Jessup and raise them up, usually two at a time. One is for our freezer locker in town so we can have our own sausages and pork chops and ham. The other is to sell at the slaughterhouse as soon as it reaches market weight.

Ben was wanting to earn his own spending money. That spring, before Mama died, Papa had allowed as how we could get a third pig to sell at the fair if Ben would agree to take on the chores of feeding and watering all three.

I had ridden along when they went to pick out the piglets. I liked to see them rooting around on the sows, making their little grunts and squeaks. Mr. Jessup always seemed to have a brand new litter of tiny, tiny ones on that farm. The first few days are the only time in a pig's life when any part of it feels soft when you pet it. I took care not to let them bite me. I like pigs when they're little, but I watch out for their teeth when I touch their wiggly pink snouts. Even their milk teeth are needle sharp, and they bite if you give them a chance. Pigs aren't mean-spirited—they're just born to bite at things. They can't help how they are.

We had taken along three burlap feed sacks. Papa has a way where he could flip a little piglet upside down with one hand and hold onto one hind leg with the other, but in general, a pig is not an animal you can hang on to very well. They will run out of our truck and into the woods if given the opportunity. We took each one home in its own gunny sack to make sure they stayed put.

On our farm we don't usually name any animals that are intended for the table. Papa asked Mr. Jessup to notch one ear of the pig Ben chose for the fair. Mr. Jessup would notch them any way you wanted or not at all if you didn't need to tell the animals apart. He has a special pair of pliers that cuts the edge of the ears. He says pigs don't have nerves in their ears and that it doesn't hurt them. I'm not so sure about that. Anyway, it doesn't make them bleed, and it doesn't matter to Mr. Jessup how anyone keeps track of their pigs as long as they pay for them.

Papa keeps a special measuring tape in our barn. When he puts it around a pig's middle, it tells him about how much the pig weighs. As soon as it gets big enough, he says it's finished off and ready for market. A sow is different from a market-sized hog, which was as big as we ever let them get at our place. For one thing a sow is huge. One of Mr. Jessup's mama pigs looks almost the size of the sofa in our parlor. He has mamas all over the place with their little ones trotting after them, squealing and rooting on them for milk. He also keeps his own big old boar in a separate pen off to the side. Even Ben is scared of that boar, though I doubt he'd admit it.

Since a pig's neck is bigger around than its head, you can't put a rope or even a collar on it to lead the animal around the way you can get a calf or a lamb to go where you want or to stay when you want it to stay. By August, to get his pig ready to take to the fair, Ben had to train it to mind.

Ben worked with his pig day after day. He took it out into our lane and used a bamboo cane to touch it gently here and there, first on one side along the flank, then on the other, training it which way to go and how to walk in the right direction. Standing in the sun, Ben would rub his pig under its tummy with the crook of the cane when he wanted it to stay still. It seemed to know what Ben wanted. He said pigs would cooperate if you don't try to rush them into anything and if you're always even-tempered and gentle. They also like to have their backs scratched. That calms them, but it wasn't something Ben could do while standing in the ring with the livestock judges breathing down his neck. When it was his turn at the fair, it was important that his animal would stay put and not wander off into the crowd of onlookers. Otherwise, he wouldn't get a ribbon.

I like pigs when they're little, but by the time Ben

had his out for training, that animal was not what anyone would call cute. I had no desire to touch its snout,
although I did like how its feet still looked as if they
were up on high heels.

"What do the judges look for?" I asked Ben. I sat
on an overturned milk crate and hugged my knees to
myself while I watched him. The sky felt yellow with
heat. There were thunderstorms to the south of us.

"Oh, I dunno. They look at everything I guess. Like
how they stand and where they carry their weight. I
think they count the nipples."

"Count the nipples?" That seemed pretty funny.

"Yeah. You want two long rows of 'em. Sixteen is
best, from what I hear."

"Why is that?" I said.

"Well, if a sow births more young than she's got
spouts, what're they all going to do for chow? I mean,
if you've got fourteen piglets but only twelve dinner
plates, it doesn't take a genius to figure that two of 'em
will turn out to be runts, and that's not good farming."

I guessed that was like not having enough chairs at
your table for everyone in your family to sit down to
supper. Our problem was having one extra chair after
our mama died.

Thinking about that vacant chair suddenly ate away
at me out there in that bright sunshine with Ben and

his pig. It came to me that no one had dared to sit at Mama's place at the table.

Ben had his pig going back and forth. He called out, "Lookit here, Katy Sue. I got 'er going."

But I didn't care about Ben's pig right at that moment. My mind had suddenly swallowed itself into how I would never ever see my mother again except in my dreams. I turned away so my brother wouldn't see that I was crying. I wondered whether, when I became a grown-up lady, I would be gentle and kind like her. I tried to picture myself in her apron, sitting down to a supper I had made. I was no longer aware of Ben or his pig going back and forth. I lost myself in a blanket of sadness, like falling into a dark pool and not knowing where the bottom is.

I wondered who might ever sit in Mama's place again. Aunt Katherine always sat across from Ben. Mama had always sat at the end of the table nearest the stove. Ingrid and I sat next to her, to help with the setting up and the clearing off.

Mama had always asked the blessing at supper. We'd settle in and wait while she decided what she'd say that particular night. She never prayed to the Lord or talked about Jesus when she said grace. She'd straighten her apron, then maybe she'd say that she'd seen a mother touch her baby real sweet, or, if we had company, she'd say how important friends are in life. Sometimes she'd give thanks that one of us kids had gotten over being sick, or that the crops had come in easy. Papa would sometimes say, "That's nice, Edna; we're a lucky family."

Ben didn't used to like how we said the blessing at our table. His friend Ronald's dad always said something written by their church, and it was over fast. My friend Alma's family just started eating, as soon as they sat down, without bowing their heads or anything. After the meningitis took Mama away, Ben admitted that he missed how she had prayed for us.

I couldn't forget those days. They came back to me no matter what I might be doing—gathering the eggs or talking to the calves, or watching Ben being caught up in what you'd look for in a good pig.

Ben's pig was still going this way and that.

"Do you remember what Mama looked like?" I asked.

"'Course I do. She looked like Aunt Katherine." Ben headed his pig off from going toward the barn.

"That's baloney," I said. "They didn't look at all alike. Not ever." I scooped up the cat. "C'mon, Clementine. Let's you and me see if the hens have laid anymore eggs."

THIRTEEN

There were only three more eggs to add to the thirteen I'd collected earlier that morning. I marked them down in the book and cleaned them with a rag I keep in the henhouse. I added two eggs to a carton that already held ten, closed it, and started the next dozen with the remaining egg.

My chore is taking care of the chickens and doing the sums on a paper where neighbors and people from town mark down that they've bought eggs from us. I also keep the pencil sharp. It hangs by a string on a thumbtack next to the paper, which is held up with more thumbtacks, a red one and a yellow one. Customers draw an up-and-down line next to their name for every dozen they take. After four dozen they draw a line across. That means five, and that's usually when they leave money in the box on the shelf, because that adds up to an even dollar. Then they scribble through all their marks they've paid for. The next time they come for eggs they start a fresh place after their name. We ask everyone to return their empty cartons. That way we always have enough.

I usually notice when people come in for eggs. I might see them from the kitchen window or the hayloft or up in the cherry tree. Once they're back in their cars, I try to guess whether they've paid. After they drive away, I go into the henhouse and check. I count the money, if there is some. Then I write down the amount in a cashbook and turn it over to Papa, although I always leave some coins in the box in case the next people need to make change for themselves. Sometimes, Papa has to remind someone to square their account with us. He calls that *settling up*. Once in a while Papa gives me back a nickel out of the egg money, although I'm not allowed to spend it on candy. That was Mama's rule.

When I stepped out of the henhouse, I saw that Ben had backed up the truck. He had the tailgate down and a big, heavy plank against it so his pig could practice walking up it and into the bed of the truck.

But the pig wouldn't go.

Papa came in from the fields. He noticed Ben pushing at the pig and treating it roughly.

"You mustn't strike your animal, Ben," Papa said. "No living thing ever learns a good lesson as a result of mistreatment. You hear what I'm saying?"

"Yes, sir."

"Now, if you just allow yourself to get the rhythm of where the critter wants to go—" Papa took up Ben's cane and guided the pig in a circle next to the truck, "—and then pick up on that rhythm yourself and guide it. . . . That's it," he said, "that's it, big fella. Now, upsy-daisy." Once Papa got the pig halfway up Ben's plank, it had no place to turn around and nowhere else to go but on into the truck. Papa quickly dropped the plank to the ground and closed up the tailgate. Ben's pig looked surprised but not unhappy. More curious than any-thing, like *how did I wind up here, for goodness' sake?*

"You'll both get the hang of it," Papa said, "like with everything, just give it the time that it needs. Take it at its own pace." He handed the cane back to Ben. "'Long as you remember there're two of you working at this. You and the pig together." Papa walked off toward the barn.

Ben let the tailgate down. The pig came to the edge and looked over, not knowing quite what to do next. Ben rescued it with the plank. He guided the animal out of the truck and back toward its shed to wait for the next practice time.

Just then the gravel in our lane crunched under some-one's tires. I turned around to see that it was our post-man, Mr. Finnegan. He drives down to the house only when there's a package to deliver. Otherwise, he leaves our mail in the box at the county road.

"Parcel post for Charles Hanson," he said, waving out the window. Papa sometimes orders parts for the tractor, but the package the postman handed me wasn't from the catalog store. It was wrapped in brown paper and tied in white cotton string. It was bigger than a boot box, but not heavy like the farm equipment we usually get. Ben came forward to sign the form that says someone responsible received the delivery.

A blue and white mailing sticker was printed with the name and address of the museum where Jake works. "This is from our friend Jake," I told the post-man. "He lives all the way back East, but he used to live out here."

"Well, that's just dandy, Katy Sue," Mr. Finnegan said. "You tell your Daddy I said to say hello, would you?"

I said I surely would, and he drove away.

"What do you think is inside?" I asked Ben.

"How should I know?" he said. "Papa's in the barn."

By then Aunt Katherine and Ingrid had come out of the house. We all gathered on the kitchen steps. Papa took out his pocketknife and cut through the string. He folded his knife and put it back in his pocket. I wished he wasn't so careful all the time. I wanted to see what was inside the package.

Papa tore off the brown paper. There was more string inside, holding on the lid of a pasteboard box. Again he took out his pocketknife and opened the blade. He sat on the next-to-the-bottom step and cut the second string upward so he wouldn't pierce anything inside the box.

"What's inside, Papa? What's inside?" I said.

"Hold your horses, there, Katydid. We'll know in good time."

He lifted off the white cardboard lid. We could see nothing but excelsior. Those wood shavings told us that whatever Jake had sent must be delicate, because that's what people use when they don't want things to break. Papa felt through the excelsior as if it, too, might break. I could hardly stand to wait. Inside was *another* box. Papa eased it out of all the wrapping and set the wrapping aside. He seemed to be paying more attention to the package than to finding out what Jake had sent us.

"Papa, what's—"

"Hush! Katy Sue. Mercy!"

Ingrid put her arm around my shoulders and drew me back. She's always more patient than me. Aunt

Katherine patted her apron for me to come to the upper step and sit in her lap. I leaned my head against her.

"Well, I'll be jiggered," Papa said slowly. I could only see the back of him where he sat on the steps below me. "Son of a *gun*!" I couldn't see through his shoulders to what he held, but his laugh echoed off the barn and bounced back on us. We all stood up and crowded around in front of him.

Papa held up a small wooden plaque cut in the shape of a shield and edged in ripples. On it was the head of a bird mounted like a hunting trophy. Underneath was a rectangle of brass with writing on it.

"What's it say?" I said. "What's it say?"

Papa held the plaque to where the light fell across the words. They were engraved to look like old-fashioned printing.

"It says, *Cor-vus vul-gar-is,*" Papa sounded the words out. "Katherine? What's that mean? *Corvus vulgaris?*"

"Well, *vulgaris* is Latin for 'common,'" she said. "And I think *corvus* is the scientific name for a crow. *Corvus vulgaris.* That would mean 'common crow.'"

"That's our crow, Papa! That's our *crow!*" I said. "The one you shot for the wager."

"Well, I'll be jiggered. It surely must be. That Jacobs is always up to something. We'll have to find a place of honor on our wall." He held it up and admired it. He shook his head slowly, "How do you suppose he knew the one I shot from the one he shot?"

"He *said* you'd laugh when it came back, Papa. That's what he said." I felt like jumping up and down.

Ben touched the glass eyes and the pointy beak. The bird's mouth was open as if it might caw. A waxy red tongue showing inside made it look as if the crow were alive, but, of course, it was only the head, after all.

Ben asked whether there wasn't a letter tucked into the package. Ingrid poked through all the excelsior and the papers and the boxes. "Nothing," she said. "Just the packing."

By then it was time for our noonday meal. There was cold sliced meatloaf from the night before and green beans and cabbage salad and cornbread left from break-fast. I knew for a fact that Papa didn't like onion in his meatloaf, and Aunt Katherine made it practically half onion, but Papa would never have let on that it wasn't to his liking.

"Dear Lord," Papa said, when we were all at the table, "we thank thee for our bounty and for the food which we are about to receive. Please forgive us our occasional impatience with one another." He paused.

"And impatience with you, too, I guess." I was surprised to hear him admit aggravation with the Lord. He started again, "We are all trying to do our best." That was when he looked straight at me and winked, although we're supposed to be looking at our plates during the blessing, and I felt bad for being caught. He took a deep, serious breath and looked back down. "We thank thee for our friendship with Hamilton Jacobs and ask your blessing on him." He paused. "And a blessing on his sense of humor, too, I guess. We are grateful for the moments of levity that you bring into our lives. Amen."

"What's 'levity' mean?" I asked. I'd never known Papa to deliver such a long grace.

"'Levity' means a sense of joy, Katydid," Papa said. "Something that makes you laugh out loud. Take some of those beans, there, and pass them along, would you please?" and for just a tiny instant, it felt as if Mama might walk in the door and sit down to join us.

FOURTEEN

*B*efore Papa and Ben went back out to the fields that afternoon, the crow's head went up on the wall by our pendulum clock in the kitchen. For a few days everyone laughed whenever somebody looked at it—such a silly thing, so small next to our big grandfather clock.

"They make clocks in Germany with little birds that come out to signal the hour," Aunt Katherine said. "Cuckoo birds."

"Real birds?" I asked.

"No, no. Carved of wood. Germans make a great many things of wood," she said. Then she took both of my hands in hers and looked into my face. "Katy Sue? Did you know Uncle Emmett and Aunt Patsy are going to have another baby?"

"Papa told me."

"Yes. They'll need help at first. Just as I helped your mama when you were born."

"Papa said I had the colic."

"You surely did."

"Papa said you held me."

"You were a beautiful child right from the start. Anyway, I talked it over with Charles—your papa, that is. We've agreed that I'll go help Aunt Patsy."

"You're going to go away?"

"It'll only be for two or three weeks. We thought— your papa and I—we thought this would be as good a time as any for me to tie things up in Chesterton. I left in such a flurry."

"You'll miss the county fair," I said.

"I know. And the start of school."

"And my birthday."

"I wish I could be in two places at once. Ingrid will have to make your cake."

The real person I wanted making my cake was Mama. I didn't want to have my birthday that year. I even hoped it would never come.

I told Aunt Katherine I would miss her. There had been times that summer when I wasn't sure I wanted her to be an inside part of our family. Then, with the thought of her going away, it seemed as if everything would feel hard and gray again. Papa said we all have to endure whatever comes our way.

Before she left, Aunt Katherine set a picture of herself as a girl with Mama on the table between Ingrid's bed and mine. And then she was gone.

☙

A few days later a man came to the door asking if Papa might want some help around the place. That time of the year, it's not unusual for men to come around people's farms looking for work. I thought Papa would turn him away like always when men wanted to hire on, but seeing as how harvesttime was coming up, and Ingrid and I had to do the kitchen work with Aunt Katherine on her visit, Papa told the man he could stay and cut the winter wood. I fetched a blanket from the cedar chest and Papa showed the man where he could keep himself out in the shed. He shook Papa's hand and said, "You won't regret this, sir." He saw me watching him and he winked.

The man's name was Alvin. He wasn't as old as Papa, but his hair was white as white could be. His eyes were milky blue and small in his face. Even in the late summer heat, Alvin wore a brown brim hat and, as he built up the woodpile, his shirt soaked through with sweat.

From the kitchen, Ingrid and I could hear the thud of the ax and the musical sound that dry wood makes when it bounces on itself. When Papa came in for supper, he told Ingrid to fix a pan of soap and water and put it on the back porch for Alvin to wash himself. Then asked her to make a plate of food for Alvin to eat in the shed.

Ingrid was doing her best in the kitchen, back on her own again. A batch of her muffins came out runny in the center and cracked on top. She made pickles, but they went so mushy we had to throw them out. The house sounded blank. I missed Aunt Katherine almost as much as I missed Mama. No one ever sat in the chair nearest the stove. Papa tried to ask the blessings, but his face was empty, and his eyes had a bony look.

After Alvin finished putting up our wood, he patched shingles on the house and fixed the fence by the pond where the heifers had been getting out. He helped slaughter one of our pigs and then rode into town with Papa to where we keep meat in the freezer locker. One night, Papa rolled Alvin a cigarette and they smoked together on the front porch after supper. Later, Papa sat alone and looked out over the fields. His skin looked lavender in the dusk.

One Saturday when Papa was winding the clock, I said I thought Alvin's white hair was like an angel's, and Papa told me Alvin must be an albino. He said someone back in Alvin's family probably looked the same.

"Does that mean something's wrong with him?" I asked.

"No, Katy Sue. It just means that's how he is. Some boys get hives when they eat cucumbers, like Ben; some girls are pretty little brunettes like you; and some people are albinos like Alvin. That's why he wears his hat all the time. Alvin can't take the sun."

Alvin seemed happy. He sang about riding freight trains and about prisoners with hard luck. I liked the song about a rock candy mountain. On the afternoon before my birthday he stopped his whistling when he caught me coming into the kitchen from the henhouse.

"What'cha got there, little Katydid?" he said, fishing a pullet egg out of my basket. "You won't be needin' this little bitty one no more, will you?" and he held it up to me between his thumb and middle finger.

"Well, . . ." I said, thinking about the cake Ingrid was going to make for my birthday.

Alvin moved one hand in front of that brown pullet egg, and when he moved his hand away, the egg was gone. He showed me both his hands and turned them over twice. No egg. Alvin stood big against the sky. I squinted up into his face and saw that he was smiling.

"Where's my egg, Alvin? Ingrid'll be needing all the extra eggs for my cake."

Alvin laughed. He removed his hat, tipped his head

forward and caught the egg in his hat. I could see his scalp was pink beneath his white hair.

"How'd you do that?"

"Magic," he said. "Pure magic." Then he put the egg back in my basket and went off whistling.

Having my birthday that year wasn't so bad after all. Ben gave me some new yellow socks, and in the morning Papa put my cocoa in one of the teacups painted in gold around the rim, just as Mama always did when she wanted to make any of us feel special. The saucers are so delicate and thin that if you hold one up to the window you can see daylight through it.

In the afternoon Ingrid made a spice cake with butter frosting. She lined up chocolate bits on top to make a "K" and stuck eleven candles around the edge, with another one to grow on. Papa told Alvin that he was welcome in the house for the celebration.

Ingrid fixed his plate of food and set it on the back steps for him to take out to the shed like other nights. But Alvin picked it up and came into the kitchen. He didn't know Papa meant for him to come in just for the cake. We were at the table, waiting for Ben to finish washing up. Standing in the doorway, Alvin looked even taller than he did out in the fields. The plate he held was like a tiny saucer in his wide hands. Alvin didn't know to take the extra chair across from Ben. Without a word, he pulled out the chair at Mama's place. Ingrid took in her breath. She looked at Papa.

I said, "That's where our mama always sat."

"Is that a fact?" Alvin answered.

"If you sit there, you'll be having to ask the blessing," I said.

"Is that a fact?" Alvin set his plate down and settled in.

Alvin's body was strong. Up close, his hands seemed as big as the skillet we fried our sausages in. He took up Ingrid's hand and reached out to me. I had never touched Alvin before. His pale skin felt warm and safe. Next thing I knew, Papa was taking up Ben's hand and stretching out for my other one.

"Our heavenly Father," Alvin started, "bless this food for which we have toiled, bless this little birthday child here, and help her grow up straight and tall, and bless this family with what they need to feel the morning sun. Amen." We all said amen and Papa thanked him. Alvin winked at me and said, "I had a mama once."

Ingrid had fixed pork chops with applesauce. We had creamed potatoes and baked squash with cinnamon and brown sugar. Ingrid's cake was good enough to take a ribbon at the fair. She'd put walnuts inside it.

Papa had seconds. After supper, Papa took up his fiddle for the first time in a long while. Alvin knew the words to most all of our songs.

What we learned from Alvin was that the house wouldn't fall in on us and the sky wouldn't crack open if someone sat in Mama's place in the kitchen. We knew she was gone whether or not we used her things or tiptoed around or changed how the furniture was arranged. Nothing would bring her back to join us again. The day after my birthday Ingrid took up Mama's place, and Papa scooted around the corner across from Ben. No one said anything. It just happened.

Then one day, Papa found me picking beans. Out of the blue he said, "Alvin will be moving on today. Just so you know to say good-bye before he goes." I followed Papa inside. He went to the cupboard and took down the box where he kept his money. He took out some bills and folded them into the pocket of his overalls. Then he went to the cedar chest and took out his old coat.

"What's he want that for on a warm day like this?" I asked.

"Winter's not all that far away."

"Where's Alvin going to go?"

"Oh, I expect he'll find more work. He's a good man."

"Can't he stay on here, Papa?" But the answer was no, and I knew not to pester.

In the yard, Alvin had his things rolled up and tied with a length of sisal rope. I asked him why he had to leave. Alvin pointed to a "V" of ducks overhead.

"Well, little Katydid, I guess I'm like those birds up in the sky," he said. "It's just time for me to be flyin' south. 'Sides, there's no more wood needs splitting. You've got plenty here to keep you warm."

Papa gave him the money and the worn-out coat. He told Alvin if he ever traveled through our way again, there'd always be something for him to eat and a place for him to sleep.

I ran into the henhouse and picked up a green and black rooster feather I'd been saving. "Here, Alvin," I said, "this will help you fly." He stood the feather in the band of his hat next to the tattered yellow one his hat must have come with. He shook Papa's hand, and then he pulled an egg out from behind my ear and handed it to me, laughing.

Alvin walked away singing and walking his bouncy walk. "Oh, the buzzin' of the bees in the peppermint trees, near the soda water fountain . . . ," until the sound grew too small to hear. Ben had come out to say good-bye and Ingrid had given Alvin a bag with sand-wiches in it. We all watched him go. Pretty soon there was just thistledown blowing across the road where he had been. We hadn't learned much about that man, like where he came from or who his people were. We didn't even know which way he turned when he came to the end of our road.

Right at that minute I missed Mama worse than ever. I missed Aunt Katherine, too.

FIFTEEN

The day came for Ben to load up his special pig for the 4-H auction at the county fair. It weighed two hundred pounds by then, according to Papa's special hog tape. Even at that size it trotted right up the plank and into the back of the truck the way it had been trained to do. That left one last pig in the shed all by its lonesome, but not for long, being as how that one would be sold at the slaughterhouse on the other side of town and would become some other family's sausages. We don't keep pigs through the winter.

Ben stayed over at the fair for two nights. All the older 4-H kids always sleep in the barns to keep their animals clean and fed until they're sold and taken away. Our house was quiet with him gone, especially with Aunt Katherine away too.

Papa took Ingrid and me to see the fair on the last day. That's when the rodeo is usually held. Papa likes to watch the calf roping, but Ingrid and I were allowed to go off on our own.

Ordinarily, I look forward to the fair, but that year it just seemed dusty and tiresome, with hawkers wanting us to buy tries on a raffle and some man who would guess your weight and give you a stuffed poodle if he was wrong by more than ten pounds. But his stuffed poodles looked dumb and I didn't care if he knew how much I weighed, anyway. I thought about buying myself a hot dog, but I wasn't hungry. I didn't even buy any cotton candy.

So much had happened in our family over the last few months that I couldn't enjoy the fair. I would rather have just had us all at home for the day—me and Aunt Katherine and Papa and Ben and Ingrid. Of course, I would have had Mama there, too, if I could. And maybe Alvin. And maybe Jake.

Ingrid met up with Cindy Sullivan from school, and the two of them dragged me around wherever they wanted to go, like to look at the quilt display and the Grange displays of different grains and pro-duce or eggs that people had raised. Then Ingrid and Cindy wanted to watch boys trying out their aim at the dime-in-a-dish stand, where if they pitched three dimes into the same dish, they'd win some stupid prize. None of the boys we watched got any dimes in, and people say those glass dishes are greased so the dimes will skip out, anyway.

Finally, Papa met up with us and bought us each an ear of corn on a stick and a hamburger with wilted onions. I scraped the onions off mine. Then Cindy found her parents and it was time to collect Ben and his things from the pig barn and go home.

He'd gotten only a green ribbon for third place, but he was happy that the man who bought his pig was going to keep it for breeding stock and not for slaughter, being as how she was on her way to being a sow. Most of the 4-H auction animals are bought for butchering.

Ben looked back at the empty pen on our way out and paused. I thought he might have forgotten some bucket or scrub brush or something and had to go back for it. But all of a sudden my brother's face crumpled up in sobbing.

"What is it, son?" Papa said. He looked alarmed. You don't ordinarily see a boy Ben's age crying unless it's really serious, especially where people might be around to see him. I guessed he couldn't help it, though, that he was overcome with missing his pig.

"She'll never know, will she?" he choked out.

"The pig?" Papa sounded bewildered.

"No," Ben cried. "Not the pig. *Mama.* She'll never, ever *know.*" He crouched his elbows to his knees as if he was in pain and another wail squeezed out of him.

Papa took Ben into a hug. Ben's arms hung limp at his sides. Ingrid took one of his hands in hers. I took up his other and patted his plaid shirt with little pats.

"Mama will never know how much we miss her," Ben was still crying, but he'd straightened himself.

Papa turned us all toward the door at the far end of the barn and walked with one arm across Ben's shoulders. "No, son, she won't. Or at least she won't know what we're all feeling now. But she knew we loved her with all our hearts. She'll always know that."

I asked, "Did giving up your pig make you miss Mama, Ben? Is that what happened?" After all, he'd raised it from when it was tiny. But Papa shushed me in a quiet way.

It was dark when we reached the house. Aunt Katherine was still in Chesterton. Aunt Patsy's baby had turned out to be twins, so she needed plenty of help for a good long while. After the babies had been born, Papa telephoned long distance to say congratulations, even though he wasn't related by blood. Uncle Emmett was Aunt Katherine's littlest brother and he was Mama's brother, too. Papa said we were all family, no matter what.

After the fair, it was time for school to start. Being a good reader, I was put into Mrs. Sturdevant's classroom. Ingrid and I packed the lunch pails early that first morning. She and Ben and I walked up our lane to catch the bus at the county road. Seeing as he had to help with getting the hay in, though, Ben would have to take an earlier bus home in the afternoons.

Daphne's milk had dried up, so we had only Emeline fresh. Still, the co-op truck was stopping in twice a week, and the man was real friendly when he emptied out our pail, even though it wasn't much milk to sell.

It was coming up on the autumn equinox, and it seemed as if the September sun had a hard time getting up in the morning to get its job done. It wasn't long before we could crunch ice around the puddles in our road on the way up to the school bus. By the time we came home in the afternoons, though, everything felt yellow again. The bus would wait while Ingrid and I crossed safely in front of it. Then it would pull away. Sometimes we'd wave to the Griffin girls or Nancy Wilcox, if they were sitting on the side where we could see them and if they were looking out the window at us. I never waved if boys were watching.

One day after Ingrid and I got off the bus she stomped the ground near me and said, "Shadow tag!

You're it!" That's how we played tag, by touching the shadow, not the person.

I ran and ran after her, past the drainage culvert under the road and past the blackberry thicket. Her shadow slid over bumps in the lane and I couldn't catch up. Then she kept to the side of the road where her shadow ran along the ditch where it was wet. We reached the house. She dropped her lunch pail on the porch. I did the same. All the while she was screeching and laughing, "You can't catch me. You can't ever catch me. I'm like the wind."

Sometimes we pretended to lose interest. That would get the other person to calm down. Then, when they were unsuspecting, you could stomp their shadow back again, and the game started over. That time, though, Ingrid didn't let up. We were all over the orchard, with her grabbing and hanging onto tree trunks, catching her breath and laughing.

"Wait up!" I yelled. "No fair." She went this way and that around the peach tree, and the sour cherry tree, and the quince tree, which stood alone down between the orchard and our hill. Next thing I knew Ingrid was crouched behind where the old Gravenstein apple tree had gone over in the heavy snow. Papa hadn't gotten around to cutting it up for wood.

"Boo!" Ingrid leaped up with her arms out to make me scared.

"Ha!" I said, and slapped both my hands onto the trunk of that downed tree where her body blocked the sunlight. "I got you." She'd forgotten about the sun being behind her and the tree, and all the skritchy branches holding her into that little hollow where she couldn't leap away fast enough. Her shadow was practically served to me on a silver platter. "You're it." And I ran as fast as I could down the path and up the other side.

Before we knew it, we'd spiraled our way up near the linden tree, and somehow it felt wrong to yell and shriek and run around up there. We were both gasping for breath and the sun was warming us and the grasses were tan and dry and bent over in a soft way, and the next thing I knew I was sitting with my knees up under my skirt and my arms wrapped around them and Ingrid was flat on her back, looking up at the sky. Pretty soon we weren't gasping and laughing anymore.

"Do you still cry over Mama being gone?" I asked her, resting one cheek on my knees.

"Sometimes. But it's not as bad as it used to be."

"Do you miss her?"

"What do you think."

"Do you think Aunt Katherine is sweet on Papa?"

"How should I know?" Ingrid said. She raised up on one elbow.

"Do you think he's sweet on her?"

"I hope not." She flattened back down again.

I lay down like Ingrid and looked through the branches at nothing but blue. "Why do you hope not?"

"It would be unseemly, with her being Mama's sister and all."

"Do you think they've ever kissed?"

"He kissed her good-bye at the train station," Ingrid said.

"I don't mean like that. Like how men and ladies kiss." I brought my arm to my lips and made a long sucking sound and ended it with a pop.

"You're disgusting," Ingrid said. "I'm going in to start supper." She stood up, tucked her blouse back into her skirt, and made like she was interested in something on the ground beside me, but what she did was find a little teeny piece of my shadow—I was still lying down—and touch it with her pinkie finger.

"Shadow tag. You're it!" and she ran away back down to the house.

By the time they brought the tractor in, Ben was crabby, with dust from the fields and little bits of dried alfalfa stuck to his sweat. Papa said it was going to be a hard winter and that they had to keep leaning into the harvest to make sure everyone had enough to eat, meaning the cows and the chickens and the heifers, who wouldn't be finished off until the next spring, and by then we'd have two more starting up. He knew the winter would be a bad one, because the woolly bears all had big fat stripes around their middles. Once when I was little, I put a woolly bear in a jar and punched holes in the lid for air and gave it some willow leaves to eat, but after a while it didn't move anymore, so I buried it beside the woodpile. I didn't know how those caterpillars could tell ahead of time what the weather would be, but I always believed what Papa said.

Papa and Ben went out again after supper, to pitch hay into the loft by lantern light. I brought my paper and crayons to the kitchen table and drew our field and put three crows on the fence wire, but I didn't think it was good enough for Mrs. Breton, so I crumpled it up and put it in the firebox of our woodstove. Ingrid tucked me in at bedtime. I was tired from running fast to catch her that afternoon. I don't know what she did before she came to bed herself. It seemed she must have rattled around with no one to keep her company in our empty house.

SIXTEEN

*T*he beginning of autumn continued like that, with Ingrid tucking me in and Ben and Papa working as long as they could into the night, and Ingrid doing her best in the kitchen on her own again.

By the time Aunt Patsy could take care of her new baby twins by herself and Aunt Katherine finally returned, we were up to our ears in the harvest. There were beans to put up in jars, and tomatoes and sweet corn. There was applesauce to make and pears to core and peel and pack into quarts. There were hard squashes to line up on the shelf in the cellar and carrots to pull and wash and bury in their box of sand so they wouldn't shrivel. We had cabbages to trim and put under burlap feed sacks that we cut open, and there were potatoes to dig. Those we kept in a pile on the cool dirt floor, and they were good as long as we didn't let light get to them.

With the pigs all gone, no one complained anymore when I fed the carrot tops to the chickens. Of course, the hens weren't laying so much by then, and we were down to three roosters. I continued to record every egg with a mark and I kept the sums in Papa's cash book. I fed the chickens their cracked corn in the morning and gathered the eggs in the afternoons when I came home from school.

That year I'd planted one hill of pumpkins. Papa showed me how to milk feed the biggest ones by using a cotton string as a wick. With his pocketknife he cut a tiny slit in the stems. Then we dipped one end of the strings into saucers of milk and tucked the other into the slits. I had tried to remember to keep the saucers full during the height of the summer, but sometimes I forgot. The vines took up the milk faster and faster. Papa said whatever they got would be to their benefit and that I mustn't fret.

With nights getting frosty, the leaves and vines withered back to show all the orange pumpkins underneath. I was allowed to put the best ones on the edge of the front steps, and Ben tied some cornstalks together to put alongside. The Hatcher boys commented on them when they came for our cider pressing. The Hatchers live in town. Papa told me it would be good manners to let them choose a pumpkin to take with them when it came time for them to pay for their jugs of cider.

We didn't eat pumpkins. Their flesh was thin and not as flavorful as Hubbard squash for pie, although we called it pumpkin pie, not squash pie when we had it at Thanksgiving. Still, I didn't like having to give away my best and biggest ones.

I had to admit that Aunt Katherine baked better pies than Mama did and certainly better than Ingrid. For the pastry, she used lard from when Papa and Alvin rendered the fat from our pig. They'd built a fire outside and used a big old black pot that was meant only for butchering.

Aunt Katherine liked to have a piece of cheese with her wedge of apple pie. She asked whether I wanted to try mine that way, and I told her the idea made me gag. Papa thought me saying that was impudent. He sent me away from the table, and I didn't get any pie that night.

The next morning, though, I noticed a slice of pie all wrapped up in waxed paper next to my sandwich for school. Ordinarily, I didn't get any dessert in my lunch pail. Aunt Katherine, who was fussing with the collar of her dressing gown, said, "I thought you might want a treat at noon."

"Yes, ma'am," I said. Papa came in just as Ingrid and I were putting on our coats and packing up our things to walk to the school bus. He studied Ingrid's tweed coat, which no longer came down below her skirts. He noticed the same thing with mine.

"You two are getting to look like a pair of regular ragamuffins," he said. "Just look at you with your wrists poking out of your sleeves. And winter coming on. We don't want people in town saying we can't care for ourselves. Katherine? What d'you think it would take to fix up Edna's blue coat?" he said. "For Ingrid, I mean. It was almost new when Edna—"

Our aunt nudged Ingrid to turn once and be sized up. "This one is a bit snug on her, isn't it?" she said. She ran one hand across Ingrid's shoulders. "She's going to have her mother's height, no doubt." She said that more to herself than anybody, then turned to Papa. "I can take up a hem if need be. If the shoulders are big, though, I don't know. I wouldn't start her with Edna's coat unless it really fits her." She looked back at Ingrid, who stood and waited for the verdict. Aunt Katherine continued. "No sense going from one extreme to the other. You know, from too small to too big. Although it wouldn't hurt for Katy Sue to move up to Ingrid's." That's when she poked at me a bit.

I didn't want Ingrid's dumb old coat. I didn't care how small mine got. Mine had been ordered directly from the catalog, and hadn't belonged to Ingrid first. It hadn't been any cousin's, either. It seemed that everything else I wore was a hand-me-down. Shoes, even. It didn't seem fair that Ingrid might have something out of Mama's trunk and I wouldn't.

Walking out to the bus, I said, "D'you think you'd ever grow out of Mama's coat? I mean, would you get bigger than her so I could have a turn with it too?" I thought about its single gold button at the collar and how the shoulder pads would make Ingrid look like a grown-up lady.

"How am I supposed to know that? Nobody knows ahead of time how tall they're going to be."

"Think it'll make you feel sad, wearing something of hers?"

"I guess. But sad in a good sort of way." Then she said she hated the smell of mothballs, and we had to run because when we came around the curve where the willows grow in the ditch we saw the bus waiting for us.

That afternoon we found Aunt Katherine sitting at Mama's sewing machine, making a rhythm with her feet flat on the treadle. She had it turned from the wall, and light from the window poured over her shiny hair and across her shoulder.

But she wasn't stitching a coat. She'd taken out a blouse that Mama had made for herself, a yellow one with three-quarter sleeves and red rickrack trim on the collar and red buttons down the front. One sleeve was on the bed, and the other was under the needle of the Singer.

"I thought I'd cut this down for you," she said. There was a sucking sound when she talked with pins in her mouth. I was afraid a pin might find its way into her throat, but she was fine. "Here. Let me hold it up to you."

I tugged my own blouse out of the waist of my corduroy skirt and undid its buttons. I laid it on the bed next to the extra yellow sleeve and stood there shivering in my undershirt. Aunt Katherine had a crazy quilt on her bed, and the yellow material looked pretty against all those other colors.

"Here," she said. "Let's slip this on and try it. Let's see how I did using your own green one for size. Watch out for the pins." She held Mama's blouse up for me to slip into. "Never mind about the other sleeve."

Sure enough, she'd cut it down, although there was plenty of room to grow. The soft material had the smell of being with woolens in the trunk, but at the same time there was a sweetness of lavender that no one else ever smelled of but Mama. I felt important at that moment, and afraid to say anything or even move. Getting that blouse felt solemn like going to church.

Then Ingrid found us upstairs. She was eating a slice of bread and butter and had one for me with jam on it. We were always allowed to fix ourselves something when we came home after school.

"Oh, Ingrid, I took a look at the coat situation." That's how Aunt Katherine talked; everything was a "situation." "That blue coat is just yards and yards. You'd swim in it no matter how much I take it up. I'm thinking we'll have to let out your old one, and that'll do for this year. Maybe next winter you'll be more filled out." My sister looked disappointed. "But look," Aunt Katherine said, "I found this funny old pair of boots. Did you know that at one point your mama wanted to be in the rodeo?"

Ingrid sat on the edge of the bed studying the floor. She shook her head no.

Aunt Katherine said, "I remember when Edna bought these boots. Grandpa was furious about their triple stitching and their fancy style. He never did tolerate much vanity. But your mama used her own money, and what could he do? Her heart was set on that rodeo. That's where she met your papa, of course."

I ran my finger over one of the turquoise leather eagles that were set into the front of the boots. The main color was gray with red piping up and down the side seams. "Our mama wore these?" I asked.

"You bet she did. Anyway, Ingrid, why don't you have them as your own."

Ingrid reached out like she was touching gold or something. "I can have them?" she asked.

"I cleaned them up with saddle soap. Wear heavy socks, and they should fit you just fine." She ran her hand over the top of Ingrid's hair. "Don't you think you'd like to wear something of your Mama's? I'm fixing this old blouse up for Katy Sue."

After that you'd see Ingrid everywhere outside in her boots. Until then my sister hadn't spent much effort on barn chores, or watering our stock or letting them into the pasture. She didn't like outside work, and besides, she'd been Mama's prodigy in the kitchen. Oh, she'd bring peelings out for the chickens and such, but you wouldn't have said she was enthusiastic about learning the particulars of farming.

With those boots, though, I swear Ingrid looked for excuses to pretend to do a chore. It turned out she needed two pairs of socks to keep the heels from scuffing when she walked, but that didn't stop her. I'd see her in the orchard or maybe playing with Clementine, always wearing Mama's rodeo boots. If any speck of mud or manure got on one of them, she'd have it wiped off right quick. When she came inside she lined them up straight on the back porch, with the left one on the left and the right one on the right, never backward and never tipped over like Ben's.

That yellow blouse became my favorite. I made sure to wear it the day school pictures were taken. In the prints that Papa bought to send to the relatives at Christmas, you could see how the rickrack trim zigzagged around the collar and matched those red buttons, even though the photographs were black and white.

SEVENTEEN

*A*s sunlight folded itself into winter's smudge of cloud and storms, days grew short and cold on our farm. On election day, Papa took me with him and Aunt Katherine to where they voted at the town hall. He explained how President Truman wanted to keep his job for four more years and not let Mr. Dewey into the White House. The next morning we heard on the radio that Mr. Truman had won, and I was happy that my family had given him two votes. Later, Papa showed me a newspaper picture of the president waving to a big crowd. He had glasses and was wearing a very nice looking coat, which told me it was cold where he was standing.

It was cold at our place, too. It was dark when we got up and dark before supper. We did nearly all our chores by lamplight. Christmas was coming, and I'm sure none of us wanted it to happen. I didn't want to think about how things had always been before, and

I knew nothing would ever be the same as when our family had been whole.

I'd always liked Christmas, with its cinnamon and sweets, and our special ways of celebrating. I liked how I could wake up early and lie in my warm bed waiting for morning to come, when Ingrid and Ben and I could finally go downstairs and find out whether our stockings had been filled. There were always tangerines in the toes of all the socks and dimes for everyone that Mama would get at the bank to make sure they'd be shiny and new. Also, we'd have chocolate coins in gold-colored foil. We usually had hard candy in the shape of a folded ribbon, and maybe a new deck of cards or some sort of puzzle that only Papa could solve after Ingrid or I gave up. Mama would stuff a goose and lay the table with a cloth that she called her wedding linen. There was always church to go to even if it wasn't on a Sunday, and we'd have candles to burn on Christmas Eve, and everyone would sing, and maybe there'd be holly with its red berries to put by the door.

That year, though, I think everyone in our family was dreading their separate memories.

Then one December morning Ben had a good idea. He said, "I know! Let's have a topsy-turvy Christmas."

"And just what would that amount to?" Papa asked.

"We'll do everything new," Ben said, "inside out and upside down. But still be respectful of the holiday," he added quickly.

"You mean we wouldn't have a Christmas tree?" I asked, "and we wouldn't string cranberries to put around it?" I was thinking of Mama's patience with the needle and thread, and how she was careful to alternate one cranberry with one piece of popcorn even if the pieces of popcorn broke. We'd always made garlands.

"Well, we could have a tree and we could have popcorn and we could have all the basic parts," Ben said. He became excited. "But we should put them together in new ways. Like, well, I don't know, like we wouldn't put the tree in the parlor, or it wouldn't be a pine tree, it could be a—, a—, a *birch* sapling or a sycamore. Something like that."

Aunt Katherine came downstairs and joined us in the kitchen.

"What's all the fuss and flurry?" she said.

"Well, Ben here has an idea to get us past Christmas without too much looking back," Papa said, "without undue sorrow over Edna and how she always made a nice holiday for us."

Aunt Katherine pulled out a chair to join us. It was Mama's chair—well, it hadn't been her chair since Alvin had sat there, and sometimes Ingrid and I would take turns, although sitting in that chair meant having to be on our best behavior.

"What's your solution, Ben?" Aunt Katherine asked.

"Well, the way I see it—"

"He wants a topsy-turvy Christmas," I broke in. Papa gave me a look for interrupting, and held his finger to his lips.

Ben began again. "The way I see it, people like Christmas for its traditions. Doing everything the same as always. Only we can't have everything the same with Mama gone."

Aunt Katherine said, "I'm not sure I'm following you."

"Well, if we make it a point to do everything different," Ben said, "we won't have to worry about—well, you know. I mean, we could have a—, a—, a *picnic!* or, uh— I know! We could all take in the *picture show!*"

"Yes, Papa!" Ingrid chimed in. "There's a new picture showing, and it's in color!"

"*The Red Shoes! The Red Shoes,*" I said, and twirled around the kitchen. I'd seen in *Look* magazine how it was a moving picture about a ballet dancer.

"Hold it, hold it, hold it," Papa said. He held his palms out like brakes on the conversation, and I stopped my twirling. "Let's don't take Ben's idea too far. I can't see the four of us—" he looked over my head toward Aunt Katherine and corrected himself, "I can't see the *five* of us taking in the moving pictures on the Lord's day."

"Okay, maybe not that," Ben said, "but do you get my point?"

"We could have Christmas with Daphne and Emeline!" I said. "Like in the Bible." I looked at Papa to see whether he liked my idea. Ingrid rolled her eyes.

Papa took his watch out of his overalls pocket and compared it to where the pendulum clock pointed. "Ben might be on to something here," he said, "but for now the chickens are waiting, and these breakfast plates aren't washing themselves."

We all gathered ourselves up to move the morning along. My head danced with Ben's idea, thinking of ways to have fun on a day that I hadn't thought would be fun at all.

In the meantime I had presents to get together. For Ingrid and Aunt Katherine I bought two small bottles of almond-scented hand cream at Rexall Drugs. For Ben I found a rabbit's foot on a brass chain for his tractor key. For Papa, Aunt Katherine helped me make a batch of old-fashioned peanut brittle. I bought the peanuts with my own money.

Aunt Katherine had to help, because to make peanut brittle you have to use very high heat on the stove. She scooted a chair over to make me tall enough to stir the pan and then tied an apron around me, up high under my armpits. First, I put two cups of sugar into our cast-iron skillet. It took a few minutes before anything happened, and I worried because the sugar still looked like sugar even though I could feel the heat in the pan. Then lumps formed in the sugar and I thought I'd made a mistake.

"Don't worry," Aunt Katherine said. "You're doing just fine." She took the wooden spoon from me for a minute and stirred to get a feel of it. After a few more minutes part of the sugar turned to syrup, golden brown. "Keep going," she said. "This is the most important part." While I stirred, Aunt Katherine buttered a flat pan to receive the hot brittle when the time came.

The stove's heat made bits of my hair stick to my forehead. My arm grew tired, but I kept stir-ring. Eventually, all the sugar turned to syrup. Aunt Katherine had my peanuts ready.

"Okay," she said, "this is when things have to hap-pen fast. We don't want to burn it." She measured half a teaspoon of baking soda and added that to my melted sugar. Immediately, the clear syrup foamed up and was no longer transparent. Next came the peanuts. I coated each and every nut and took care not to let anything stick to the bottom of that heavy black skillet.

"It's ready," Aunt Katherine said. She took hold of the pan with a doubled pot holder and poured the brittle onto our buttered pan. "When it's cool, you'll need to break it apart into pieces," she said. "If we're lucky, a few bits will fall off. We'll have to eat those as samples." She smiled. "You do like peanut brittle, don't you?"

"Are you kidding?" I said. "I like it more than anybody."

Of course, I was responsible for washing the pans and utensils, since it was my present to Papa. When I asked if we could have watermelon for Christmas Day, Aunt Katherine said she didn't think you could find a place to buy watermelon in the winter and even if you could, the price would be sky high.

By the time Christmas finally came, we were all excited with our adventure. I woke up early that morning and lay in bed wondering how everything would work out. I hadn't put out a sock; I'd put out my knit hat. Other than that Ben had made me promise to leave all the topsy-turvyness to him and Aunt Katherine. They wanted everything to be a surprise. With the gray of dawn, I could make out the bare branches of the cherry tree outside my window. I whispered, "Ingrid. Are you awake yet?"

"Shhh," she mumbled and rolled over, "I'm still sleeping."

"If you're talking you can't be sleeping," I said.

"Merry Christmas, then."

I heard someone go down the stairs. It was either Aunt Katherine or Ben. With Papa using the down-stairs room, I couldn't tell if he was awake. The toilet flushed. Something clattered in the kitchen. Then I heard Papa's laugh come up through the floor, and I knew for certain it wasn't too early to get up.

"Come on, Ingrid," I said. "We can go downstairs now. It's Christmas." I was still whispering, although I didn't know why. Everyone was awake.

In the kitchen, Aunt Katherine was in her dressing gown. On the stove she had a pan of hot cider with cin-namon sticks and cloves in it. We'd always had cocoa.

"Merry Christmas!" she said, and she handed us each a small basket. I looked at Ingrid to see if she knew what we were supposed to do. "Go on into the parlor and see what you can find," Aunt Katherine said. She bubbled over with smiles, and Papa winked at her.

It being early morning, Ben's voice was croaking. "Hey," he said, "there's a tangerine behind the lamp." And sure enough, there was one, shiny and fragrant.

My knit cap was as empty as when I'd laid it out the night before. But I spied two chocolate coins whose edges peeked out from under the corner of the rug. I picked them up and put them in my basket. "I get it!" I said. "It's like Easter." Ingrid picked up another tangerine from behind the sofa. Just then I looked up and saw a wrapped present on the high shelf where we keep a figurine of a lady in a big dress.

There were mittens that Aunt Katherine had knit for everyone, and new coats for Ingrid and me. There was a big jigsaw puzzle with a picture of horses pulling a wagon through a covered bridge in autumn. And there was a book about birds for Ben.

"That's so you can keep up with Jake," Papa said. Ben was anxious to go out walking later in the day to try to identify as many birds as he could.

Papa was surprised that I'd made peanut brittle. "All by yourself?" he asked.

"Almost," I said, and looked at Aunt Katherine, who was smiling. "A little bird told me the recipe."

Then it was time for breakfast. We'd always had ham and eggs and a special bread with nuts and raisins. That morning, though, we were in for the biggest surprise of all. Aunt Katherine had the table set with soup bowls.

"Well, I figured there was one sure way to have a topsy-turvy breakfast," she said. "And that was to have lunch for breakfast." She turned from the stove to where we sat, "You all like corn chowder, don't you?"

"Corn *chowder*," I said, "I *love* corn chowder!" I couldn't believe that's what we were having Christmas morning. Everyone was laughing and talking at once.

"You're a good sport, Katherine," Papa said, "a real good sport." He raised his cup of hot cider. "Let's all give three cheers for Katherine, shall we?"

Later in the day Ingrid said I was supposed to help her and Ben move our table and chairs out to the barn.

"To the *barn!*" I said. "What on earth for?"

"Because you had the bright idea of having Christmas dinner with the cows," she said. "It's going to be a picnic."

And sure enough, Ben had made a fire in the pot-bellied stove and lit the kerosene lamps. Aunt Katherine had added some candles in holders that she'd made out of bright red apples. We had slices of roast beef and beet salad and mashed potatoes and quince jelly for our biscuits. There was a pitcher of lemonade and more hot cider. In the middle of eating, Papa realized he'd forgotten to ask the blessing. Then he allowed as how he guessed we were already blessed by Ben's good idea and Aunt Katherine's willingness to go along, and with Ingrid and me letting everything come as a surprise and then helping with things around the edges.

That night after dishes were put away back in the house and all was tidied up, Ingrid and I were working the new jigsaw puzzle. I had just fit in the last of the corner pieces when Papa burst in from outside. It had started to snow and his heavy jacket was white across the shoulders.

"I need your help in the barn, Ben," he said, "Daphne's calf is coming. She's laboring hard and fast. You girls can come watch if you want, but wear your old coats. It's bound to get messy."

We bundled up. Ingrid put on Mama's gray boots. I found my heavy socks and asked Aunt Katherine if it would be okay to wear my new mittens.

"Better not," she said. "Not if you want to pet the new calf after Daphne licks it clean."

By the time Ingrid and Aunt Katherine and I made it out to the barn, Daphne was already lying on her side and laboring. Huffing and pushing.

"Looks like it's coming fast," Papa said. "Stand back."

"Must be 'cause of my lucky rabbit's foot," Ben said, and gave me a squeeze.

Next thing we knew Daphne adjusted her haunches. She made low, nickering sounds that weren't like her usual moos. Something rhythmic rippled along her big sides. She let out the longest, loudest moo I'd ever heard. A pair of front feet came into view, sticking straight out, then the pink nose, tucked against its knees. Finally, with one great big heave from Daphne, she delivered the calf onto clean straw. It wobbled its head in the puddle of afterbirth. Right away Daphne turned and cleaned the membranes free from the little animal's snout so it could start to breathe and make its tiny noises.

"Eee-yew" Ingrid said, "how can Daphne stand to lick up that goopy stuff with her *tongue?*"

"Mothers do amazing things for their young," Aunt Katherine said. "That's just how the world works." She slipped her arm around Ingrid's waist, and we watched while Ben put down clean straw and brought Daphne a bucket of fresh water. The new calf tottered onto its skinny legs and suckled for first milk. Papa said it was too soon to pet it, and he cleared us out before long, announcing it was time for bed and that he and Ben would finish cleaning up.

Soft, wet snowflakes almost as big as pullet eggs plopped on us as we stepped out into the night. On my way toward the house I tilted my head back to let the snowflakes dizzy me. I held my tongue out to the black, black falling sky.

I can't say it was the best Christmas ever, because it wasn't. Not with Mama gone. But I can say it was a day I will always remember.

EIGHTEEN

*T*he morning after Christmas day we woke to a foot and a half of snow. We wore a channel through to the henhouse and to the barn, checking on the new calf. I didn't let the chickens out into their yard, because chickens don't know what to do about snow.

After the morning chores, we were housebound. Of course, we were on school vacation, so we didn't have to worry about getting to the bus. School would have been canceled anyway.

Papa replaced the washer in the bathroom's hot water faucet so it wouldn't drip anymore. Next, he stood on a chair and dusted the top of the pendulum clock. After that, he asked Aunt Katherine whether there was any coffee left from breakfast, but after she said there was, he changed his mind. Instead he had a glass of water. I could tell he was nervous about something.

Aunt Katherine sang and hummed as she cleaned up from breakfast. She started a batch of bread rising and sliced the leftover roast for sandwiches. She put the bones in a pot on the stove to boil for soup that I supposed that would be for lunch. All the while she hummed and sang to herself. It was the sort of singing that has no particular words or tunes, but you can tell the person who's humming feels happy about some secret thing.

I drifted off to the jigsaw puzzle. Pretty soon Ingrid joined in and then Ben brought his new bird book into the parlor. All three of us were quiet, thinking our own private thoughts, I guess.

Once Papa and Aunt Katherine ran out of things to putter with, they showed up in the parlor too. It was like a holiday all over again having us all there and no outside chores or activities we could do. The only difference was that we weren't in our dress-up clothes. Ingrid and I were on the floor with the puzzle, and Ben was sitting in the rocker. Papa and Aunt Katherine were on the settee. It seemed strange that they would sit side by side. Papa cleared his throat.

"How's that puzzle coming along?" he asked.

"Fine."

He cleared his throat again. "Ben, you're liking that book, are you?"

"Yes, sir."

Papa shifted around on the settee. Finally he said, "I was going to say something yesterday, but I didn't want to step on Ben's plans for Christmas. Anyway, here we all are, aren't we, and—well? What would you kids think if your Aunt Katherine and I took up with each other?"

Ben clapped his book shut. "I knew it!" he said. He bounced his fist off his knee like it was a victory of some sort.

Ingrid drew in her breath.

"What does it mean, take up with each other?" I asked.

Ben said, "They're sweet on each other, silly."

I looked to Ingrid to see if we liked the idea, but she was just staring at them blankly.

Aunt Katherine sat forward. "I'm not going to try to take your mother's place," she said. "No one can ever do that. No one *should* ever do that. I'll still be your aunt, same as now." Her words tumbled like water over rocks and her hands flew from her mouth to her lap and back again.

Papa said, "You see, we've discovered a *fondness* for each other."

"It's just that your papa is such a good and decent man, you see," she said. Then they dared to look at each other. Papa took hold of her hand with the two of his.

I said, "You mean, like you're going to get *married?*"

Ben said, "It means they're going to be *courting*. People don't just up and get married, Katy Sue."

"Ben's got the right idea," Papa said. He sat forward a little. "We're going to take things slow, ease our way into this whole situation. Y'see, Katherine here—and me, too, I'd guess—well, we never *anticipated* any of this—"

He trailed off and the room fell silent.

Ingrid looked at the floor. "But what about—?"

"Ingrid, darling—all of you—really," Aunt Katherine said, "you won't see any changes that we won't tell you about ahead of time. We're family. First and foremost, we have your mother's memory to care for."

"But Mama's only been gone less than—" Ingrid twisted her shoelace around and around. "I mean shouldn't you—Oh, who cares about her anymore except me, anyway!" Ingrid spilled puzzle pieces and stormed up the stairs. The door to our room slammed, and I could hear her crying. Aunt Katherine started to go after Ingrid, but Papa held up his finger to suggest that she wait.

Ordinarily, no one slammed doors in our household. When Ben motioned that he was willing to follow Ingrid, Papa nodded. Nobody minded that I tagged along.

Ben knocked on our door while I stood behind in the hallway. No answer. Ingrid just kept on sobbing.

He knocked again. Still nothing. Ben looked at me and I shrugged.

Slowly, he opened our door, and I followed him in. It wasn't as if I needed permission to enter my own room.

Ben sat on Ingrid's bed and talked to her calmly and put his hand on her back and stroked the tangles out of her hair as best he could with his fingers. He didn't ask her any questions or say everything was fine. He just said soothing things like how everyone probably felt confused and there's no predicting the future. He didn't utter Mama's name, or Papa's, or Aunt Katherine's.

Ben waited until Ingrid was ready. Eventually she rolled over and looked at him and saw that I was in the room too. Her cheeks were red and splotchy.

"We have to be a team," she said, looking from Ben to me. I liked that I was included, although I didn't exactly know what she had in mind about being a team. "I mean, we have to stick together," she said, "now that we're losing Papa too." Her lower lip quivered. I thought she was going to cry again.

"What are you talking about?" I said. "We're not exactly going to become orphans."

She took a long, jerky breath and looked out the window. Her face seemed hard. Her eyes looked like two dots and her mouth was nothing more than a thin line.

Ben said, "We've always stuck together. I expect we'll do the same from here on out." He turned to me, "Right, Short Stuff?"

Usually, I don't like to be called *short stuff*, but right then it felt okay. I didn't know whether Ingrid wanted it to be us kids against the grown-ups in the house or what. I guess I was willing to go along with whatever she and Ben decided. I wasn't so sure I liked the idea either, of Papa marrying Aunt Katherine. I'd wondered if they might take up with each other, but I didn't think it would ever happen. I couldn't imagine Papa loving anyone but our mama, but I didn't like to think of him being alone and lonely all the time either.

"Hey, Ingrid," Ben said, as he nudged her bed with his knee to jiggle her to attention, "what if it weren't Aunt Katherine who Papa was sweet on but some lady from church, like Mrs. Garrison? Then we'd *really* be in the soup."

"Oh, no!" I said. "Mrs. *Garrison!*" She was that widow who kept bringing awful food to us right after the funeral. She was nice enough, but she had two truly bratty kids.

Ingrid said, "I hardly think Papa would look twice at someone like that."

"But let's try to see things from his side. Aunt Katherine's already family," Ben said.

Ingrid brightened a little. "*And* she doesn't have any bratty kids."

"Yeah, Ingrid," I said. "To Aunt Katherine, maybe *we're* the bratty kids. Ever think of *that?*"

"Just you, Katy Sue. Just you," Ingrid said, with a know-it-all smirk.

I let her have the last word. As the littlest, I was used to that.

We don't heat the upstairs of our house during the day and certainly not on a snow day like that one. The sky was so blue it made my eyes hurt, and everything sparkled underneath. It was the sort of day you knew not to touch anything metal outside. I could see Ingrid getting cold, but she didn't have the nerve to crawl under her covers, not during the middle of the day. For one thing she still had her shoes on. It was good Mama couldn't see Ingrid lying on top of her comforter without taking them off.

"Why don't we all go into the kitchen by the woodstove," Ben asked. "Papa has a nice fire going and we could have some cambric tea." That's what Mama used to fix us for comforting, with lots of milk and sugar and not much actual tea. "Maybe later we'll find some birds to identify with my book." He stood and went to the window. "Besides, Short Stuff and I are planning to bundle up for a walk in the snow," he gave me an eye, "aren't we?" I looked back at him, trying to read his face to be sure I responded the right way. I nodded.

"Yeah," I said. "It's going to be an adventure. Maybe in our new coats, huh?" I hadn't heard about any plan to go walking, but it was okay with me if that's what everyone wanted to do. Maybe we would see how the linden tree looked with snow in its branches. It seemed only right to brush off Mama's marker where all our names showed. Maybe we'd play fox and geese. Maybe Papa would join in.

By then Ingrid was sitting on the edge of her bed. "I'll agree to go down to the kitchen," she said, "but I don't want to have to talk to *her.*"

"Well, that's going to be a little bit tricky," Ben said.

"Yeah, Ingrid, where's Aunt Katherine supposed to go, anyway? You can't expect her to disappear just because you're mad at her," I said.

"I'm not *mad* at her," Ingrid said. "It's just that—it's just that—oh, *I* don't know. It's just that, I mean—Papa—how could he *do* that to us?" Then she began to cry again, and through her blubbering I made out the words as they came between gasps, "It hasn't even been a *year* since Mama died."

"We know that," I said. "C'mon. Let's all go down-stairs, so they won't feel as if we've turned against them."

NINETEEN

*I*t turned out Papa had another surprise besides him and Aunt Katherine being sweet on each other. This one came the day before New Year's Eve. He explained that two people who are courting can't live under the same roof. It isn't proper, he said. That meant Aunt Katherine had to move somewhere else while they figured out whether the two of them were going to get married. They'd already made an arrangement with our neighbors, the Culshanks.

It sounded like a silly rule of manners to me. Ingrid and Ben explained it was all because men and ladies aren't meant to do you-know-what before the wedding.

"You think Papa and Aunt Katherine are going to do *that?*" I asked. "Aren't they too old?" The three of us were again in Ingrid's and my room, but this time Ingrid wasn't upset and crying. She was realizing that

Mama was going to be gone whether Aunt Katherine was around or not, and that the house felt better when she was there. We seemed to congregate in our room more and more, though not as us-against-them, the way Ingrid had first wanted.

Ben said, "Of course they're going to do *that*. If they get married, I mean. That's what married people do."

"You don't think Papa did that with our mama do you?" I asked.

"Katy Sue," Ben rolled his eyes, "didn't anyone ever tell you the facts of life?"

Ingrid said, "Where do you think the three of us came from, anyway?"

"Well, I think it's a dumb rule," I said. "Why does Aunt Katherine have to go live with the Culshanks just because she might love our papa? I mean, you'd think that would be all the more reason for her to be *here* with us!"

No amount of explaining could make me understand.

◇

The Culshanks are our closest neighbors. They have a full quarter section that they plant in corn. Their two boys are grown and moved away, and Mr. Culshank can't work 160 acres by himself, being as he's getting on in his years. They have a hired man, Otto. Mrs. Culshank sits around the house and does needlework all day. She doesn't even grow their own tomatoes. She says the sun bothers her eyes and I guess her eyes are sort of squinty. 'Course the Culshanks buy their tomatoes from us, and eggs and peaches and everything else we have.

There's a footpath from their place to ours. It cuts through the woodlot and around the pond.

Papa made the arrangements. He and Ben moved some of Aunt Katherine's things to the spare room above the Culshank's kitchen. In return, Aunt Katherine was going to teach Mrs. Culshank how to play the piano they inherited from some relative of theirs.

Aunt Katherine was to be at our house after school and during supper and all day on Saturdays. Sundays, she would go to church with us and stay on through the midday meal. Ingrid and I had to take on doing breakfast again before school and packing all the lunches, which Ingrid didn't like doing at all.

During that January and February Aunt Katherine walked to our place every afternoon no matter what, even when the weather was bad. Sometimes she'd arrive just as Ingrid and I were coming down the lane from the school bus. With it still being winter, evenings were dark as dark can be. Papa walked Aunt Katherine back to the Culshanks' every night as soon as things were cleared up in the kitchen. I could tell by how he looked at her that he didn't want her to leave, and I'd say she didn't want to go, either. Sometimes she looked like a sick cow around her eyes—just for a minute—when she had to bundle up for her walk through the night. But then she'd find her smile again and her hands would flutter into her pockets to check for her mittens, or she'd fuss with her scarf. She might say something like, "Oh, heavens. I'd forget my head if it weren't screwed on."

If there was too much snow accumulated and drifting in the fields, they'd take the long way around, following our lane and the county road where the plow had been. That must have been when they did their actual courting. You could tell they dawdled, because sometimes Papa would come home later than you would think for the short distance he had to walk.

Naturally, we all missed Aunt Katherine. She wasn't there to tuck us in. She wasn't home to say something cheerful in the mornings. She wasn't there to settle any squabbles Ingrid and I might have about how to pack the lunches.

One morning we were in a hurry. Ingrid was slicing what was left of the Sunday roast when all of a sudden she cried out, "*Damn* it!" She popped the knuckle of her thumb into her mouth and began to wail like a banshee, which was hard to do with her thumb in her mouth.

Papa rushed in from shaving. "Here, here," he said. "What's all the caterwauling?"

Ingrid wouldn't answer.

"She cut her thumb with the carving knife," I said, "making sandwiches."

Papa eased Ingrid's hand away from her mouth to have a look. She was bleeding, but not all that badly. Normally, Ingrid doesn't go to pieces over something small like that. Papa sat her down and patted her as if the rest of her might break apart.

"Ben, would you please get us some adhesive tape and gauze from the bathroom cabinet?" he said, "I'm going to do some doctoring here on your sister. Oh," he called after, "and bring the surgical scissors too."

That made Ingrid wail all the more.

"Not for you, little dumpling," Papa said. He patted her leg and tried to get her to look at him. "For cutting the tape. That's all."

Ingrid's crying faded to a pout. She watched with ragged breaths as Papa cut a length of white tape and stuck it by one end to the edge of the table. Next, he folded a square of gauze into a little pad that he placed directly over the base of her thumb and held it tight for a few seconds before securing it higher up with the tape, which he wound around twice before trimming off the extra.

"That should keep most of your blood on the inside where it belongs," he said. "Not too tight, is it?"

"No, it's not too tight," she said, "but it's crooked. Aunt Katherine would have put it on straight." She finally raised her eyes up from the floor. Half of Papa's face was still covered with shaving lather. Though she hadn't finished pouting yet, she said, "You look funny."

"Not half as funny as you're going to look if you miss the school bus." With that Papa wiped at his cheek with a dish towel and went over to the counter to finish assembling our lunches. Never once did he admonish Ingrid about the curse word she'd used.

Because we were late to begin with and because it was cold and because Ingrid had cut herself, Papa drove us in the truck up our lane to catch the bus, which it turned out was also late that morning.

Ingrid sat by the window; I was in the middle. While we waited Ingrid fiddled with the bandage on her thumb, trying to make it look tidier. She was still sort of pouty. "I wish you and Aunt Katherine would hurry up and get married," she finally blurted out. "It was better when she wasn't just a visitor."

Papa looked startled, then pleased. But before he could put together any kind of an answer, the yellow of the bus showed through the branches. It was time for my sister and me to scramble out of the truck and join our friends in the seats they'd saved for us.

TWENTY

*W*ith Aunt Katherine staying at the Culshanks',
it didn't take long before the whole world knew about
her and Papa starting to love each other. Nevertheless,
they wanted to make it official.

Each February, around Washington's birthday, there's
always a social at the Grange hall. That year it was no
different. Mr. Harriman, the druggist, agreed to be the
square dance caller, as always. Men took their fiddles and
harmonicas, and farmers brought in bales of straw for
the musicians to sit on when they got tired of standing.

Everyone was invited, including people who aren't
members of the Grange. Mrs. Breton was there with
her husband, who works for the post office. There were
kids from school and babies and folks too old to dance.
Ingrid and I stuck together, but Ben wandered off with
the Wilcox boys. One man whose teeth were missing
sat himself against the wall the whole time and clapped
to every song, only it made no sound when his two dry
palms came together, soft as they were.

There was a long table where women put their food. There was everything you'd ever want to eat. Fried chicken and corn salad and anything you could imagine to pickle. There were biscuits and corn bread with honey to put on it, and green beans with bacon, and baked beans with molasses. There was macaroni casserole and rice with tomatoes mixed in and with cheese on the top. Someone brought hamburger hash with cream gravy, and there were platters of sliced meats and deviled eggs. From our house, we took scalloped potatoes with onion. Aunt Katherine wrapped the pot in a terry cloth towel and tucked it into a corrugated box to keep it warm until she set it out on the table when it came time to eat.

Desserts were kept separate. Every kind of pie and cake. Butterscotch pudding. Slice-and-bake cookies. Green Jell-O with pears inside. Mrs. Sturdevant set down a whole plate of fudge.

Papa had arranged ahead of time that he would ask the blessing. Before the dishing up began, Mr. Harriman tapped a spoon against a glass to quiet people down. They left off their conversations and bowed their heads. Not all the babies knew to stop their clatter, but no one minded.

Mr. Harriman held his arms up high to get everyone's attention at his end of the hall. "Welcome," he said. He had a voice that sounded like melting butter. "Tonight we are lucky to have Charles Hanson say the grace. And, I believe, he has an announcement to make." He dropped his arms and turned to Papa with a wink, "Isn't that right, Charles?" People laughed in a soft ripple like a brook washing over pebbles. Maybe some of them knew what was coming.

"Well, I—" Papa said. He sounded bashful.

Mr. Harriman looked out at the crowd. "Will that announcement be made before the blessing or after, Charles?" He turned to Papa where they stood side by side. "Folks say you're in a rush to get this news out. My guess is you'll make your announcement first?"

Papa made like he was wrestling Mr. Harriman. "Everything in good time, Eugene," he said. The two of them laughed, then straightened themselves out. "All jokes aside," Papa said to everyone. He folded one hand over the other in front of himself and bowed his head. "Bless us, O Lord, and these thy gifts which we are about to receive from thy bounty and bless them in their use and us in thy service. Amen." Then he looked up quietly and held out his hands the way Mr. Harriman had when he wanted everyone to stay in place. "One more thing," he said. The crowd stirred. "Benjamin? Ingrid? Could you please join me? Katy Sue?"

As we made our way toward him, Aunt Katherine broke away from the women she'd been standing with and joined us.

"I have one more blessing to ask," Papa said. "This one's a little more personal. I know you want to get to your supper, so I'll make it short and sweet." He took Aunt Katherine by one hand and tried to squeeze us kids in with his free arm. "Tonight I ask your blessings on my family. As you know it's been a tough year with Edna gone. I couldn't have gotten through it without the strength of my children." Papa's face reddened and his eyes became shiny. I tried to imagine that Mama was listening, but Ingrid's elbow poking into my arm distracted me. Papa swallowed hard and went on, "And there've been some changes in my household following our loss." He dropped his arm from around us and put both his hands over Aunt Katherine's.

A man in the back of the room called, "Just spit it out, Charles! Take us out of our misery."

"Well," Papa began again with a nervous laugh, "tonight I'm here to ask your blessing on Katherine and me." I could see he was choked up, almost crying. His voice cracked, and I doubt most people could hear the actual words as he said them. His voice was down to almost a whisper. "Because I have asked her to marry me, and she has said *yes.*"

Men and women whooped and cheered. There was clapping and kissing and people shaking Papa's hand. Aunt Katherine was full of bashful smiles. Ladies drew her off in a bustle of excitement. People shook my hand and smoothed my hair, as if I were getting married myself, and, in a way, I guess I was. Mrs. Garrison asked if we kids were settled in this decision, and I felt as if she were prying into our private matters.

Then it was time to eat. By the time I got to the dessert table, the fudge was all gone.

After that, Mr. Harriman began, "Swing your partner round and round . . ." and the fiddling began and the ladies swished their skirts as they danced. Papa started out partners with Aunt Katherine then he took Ingrid as his partner, and Aunt Katherine took Ben. Eventually, I had my turn with Papa.

Mama hadn't particularly liked to square dance. She said it tangled her feet around each other like vines on a fence post. But Aunt Katherine loved to dance. Her cheeks grew pink with excitement, her hair shone when it moved with her, and she looked more beautiful than ever. Not as pretty as Mama, but beautiful in her own way.

TWENTY-ONE

We flew through the month of March and came into April in a burst of wedding preparations, cleaning and straightening anything that could be cleaned or straightened. You'd have thought the king of Siam was invited. At the same time, Papa had the farming to do and the crops to think about getting in the ground. The willows along the road found their leaves again, and the cherry tree outside my window was coming back to life. It made me think of the picture I'd put in my drawer almost a year before. Since then I'd drawn lots of pictures of our family and of Aunt Katherine and of our cat Clementine and a few of our crows. I had come to appreciate crows since Jake told me about them being intelligent, and sometimes I'd talk to them when they came to our fields. I wondered how they could tell their families apart. Those birds all looked exactly the same to me.

I began to spend more time outside. The horizon looked bigger day by day. Maybe it had been that big all along, and I'd simply had no cause to look out that far into the distance.

Aunt Katherine stayed extra at our house on account of the preparations. She used Mama's sewing machine to stitch her outfit, a pink suit with white piping. Not all brides have to wear white. The hat she'd found at the dress shop was the same shade of pink as her suit. The hat had a feather sticking out of it, which made me miss Alvin and wonder whether he'd ever be coming through our way again. I'd told Aunt Katherine all about him, and I hoped she'd meet him someday.

Aunt Katherine let me try on her hat. It had a pink net that she could pull down over her face or fold up along the edge. When I looked through the net, it made blurry dots over everything.

Ingrid and I had new dresses to wear, store-bought dresses. Mine was yellow; hers was aqua, but they were cut the same, with sashes to tie at the back. We didn't have hats to wear. Aunt Katherine sewed Papa and Ben new shirts of crisp white cotton.

Aunt Katherine had a wedding cake recipe from way back in her and Mama's family. She said it was made for the day Mama married Papa and that it had been served at all the wedding celebrations in the Gilbert family. That was Aunt Katherine's maiden name, the name she'd be giving up to become a Hanson.

The cake recipe called for all manner of nuts and preserved fruits and candied peel, much like a Christmas cake only not darkened with brown sugar. Ingrid took on the responsibility of making it. We believed it would be bad luck for a bride to bake her own wedding cake, although Aunt Katherine would be helping with the icing.

Aunt Katherine thought it would be a good idea for Ingrid to practice a time or two to make sure she got the cake right. She tried it twice. With it being spring, the chickens were laying plenty of eggs, and Daphne and Emeline's milk was rich with butter. The practice cakes were small, because the rest of the ingredients were very expensive. Besides, Papa thought it might make us all sick to have to eat two huge cakes. I didn't think so, but no one asked for my opinion. Ingrid's first try was undercooked; the second try was over-cooked. Aunt Katherine, who trusted Ingrid to do a good job with the real thing, said a cake between the two would be just right.

At first, Papa thought he would ask the minister to come out to our house, and they could stand up in the parlor for the marriage ceremony. Then he realized that everybody wanted to celebrate the wedding: the relatives and people from town, the neighbors, and every-one else. Still, he wanted to get married on our place and not at the church like most people. Papa believed our land was blessed. Maybe he didn't want to leave Mama out. Whatever his reasons were, he decided the wedding would be held in our orchard.

Mrs. Culshank might not raise her own vegetables, but she was famous for tending to her big flower garden. She offered to make Aunt Katherine's bouquet. Also, she got their hired man, Otto, to hoist her spinet piano into the back of their truck and bring it over to our place for the music. Of course, Otto and his wife would be at the wedding, too.

Jake came out by train, only this time he stayed with some cousin out near Lake Augusta, so the cousin would be coming to the wedding also. Jake was to be Papa's best man. Aunt Katherine wanted to ask Ingrid and me both to stand up with her, but Papa felt we were too young, and you can't have two people sign the certificate anyway, so she asked Mrs. Culshank. When you have a married woman, you say matron of honor, not maid of honor. I don't think Aunt Katherine really wanted Mrs. Culshank, but she felt she should after living under her roof and all.

All the aunts and uncles from around Chesterton came, and all the people from town who knew Aunt Katherine and Papa, and even people who'd mostly known Mama. Early in the day our house was wild with preparations. Women in the kitchen were fixing platters of food as if they owned the place. Men were everywhere outside, moving harrows and barrels out of sight, carrying chairs outside for the older people to sit in if they couldn't stand. Someone sent a telegram from Kansas and Western Union brought it. Papa gave the man a tip.

People say it's bad luck for a groom to see his bride ahead of time on their wedding day, but that was going to be too hard to accomplish, so each time Papa and Aunt Katherine had to pass each other, they pretended not to look. Then they'd laugh.

Ben and I were in charge of the ribbons. Jake helped. He's very good at getting things to come out even. Our orchard was laid out on a square. Way back in time, our grandpa planted the trees in neat and proper rows. Aunt Katherine had chosen the two middle rows as the path she would walk down. With a whole roll of white satin ribbon as wide as the sash on my dress, Ben cut lengths and Jake helped me reach them around the trunks of our apple and pear and peach trees and tie them to make it look like a church aisle. Ben left plenty of extra when he cut the ribbons, so the ties would drape like streamers almost to the ground and stir in the breeze if we had any. The orchard was in bloom by then, so from time to time the branches would release a few blossom petals that would flutter to the ground. The bows were tied on the sides of the trees Aunt Katherine would see as she approached Papa and the minister.

Everything was set up. Aunt Katherine was upstairs, fussing with her clothes and attended by the women who wanted to help and giggle. She and Papa were going to go away for a one-night honeymoon in the lodge at Lake Purcival. She'd already packed her things, including a lace-edged nightie she had ordered from the catalog.

Ben and Jake wandered off to the barn, where men were setting up a table for the strawberry punch, made with berries from our freezer locker in town. It was too early for me to get into my dress, and I didn't have any more chores that needed doing. I guess Papa was at loose ends, too. When I saw him wander off on his own, I followed.

First, he walked down the aisle of bows, as if to make certain it was good enough. He walked slowly, with his hands in his pockets and his eyes on the ground. When he came to the end, where he could see out to the fields, he looked at the horizon for a good long while. Then he walked down the ravine and up the other side. I followed.

I thought I'd find him sitting on the large rock

that sticks out of the ground up on the hill. Instead, he was pulling weeds from around the base of Ben's yellow rosebush, which was just coming into leaf; it was too soon for flowers. Next he bent some grasses back from around Mama's marker. When he saw that I was watching, he reached out for me to sit with him on the rock.

Papa was crying, but not the excitement tears he'd had the night of the social at the Grange hall. It seemed sad that a man would have to cry on his wedding day. Eventually, he took out his big handkerchief. He offered it to me first, since I needed to wipe tears off my face too. Neither of us said anything at first. I expect we were both tangled up with our private thoughts at that point.

Up there you can see our entire place. Papa looked out and said, "This land has been ours for a long, long time, hasn't it?"

"Yes, Papa."

"I expect this land will be here forever."

"Yes, Papa." I hadn't ever thought about land going away.

He hugged me and I hugged him back. He said, "This is where our family lives, no matter what."

"Yes, Papa."

He kissed my forehead, then put his first two fingers to his lips and kissed their tips. He knelt down and touched those two fingers to Mama's marker. I did the same.

Then he surprised me. He swung me around and said, "What d'ya say we go down the hill and get ourselves ready for a *weddin'*!"

TWENTY-TWO

*A*unt Katherine looked beautiful in her new suit. She had stopped wearing bright red lipstick as soon as she learned that Papa didn't like that shade very much. She'd found a pale peachy pink at Rexall's to match her suit. Papa looked handsome in his white shirt. He and Ben wore neckties and had slicked their hair down with some goopy stuff that men use to make their hair smell spicy. Ingrid and I tied each others' sashes, making sure the bows were even, because lots of people would be looking at us from the back as we walked down the aisle.

Mrs. Culshank had made Ingrid and me corsages on elastic straps to slip over our wrists. There were so many flowers on them, the elastic barely showed through. We had lily of the valley and violets and purple heather and pink baby's breath all tied together with lavender ribbons. Aunt Katherine carried the same, but with five white tulips in the middle, their long stems hanging down with extra ribbon. On the food tables, there must have been thirty separate tiny vases of pansies of all different colors—white and purplish black and yellow and light blue. Each vase had a ribbon around it that matched the one on my wrist.

Finally, everyone had arrived. The piano music started, and Ingrid and I were first to go down the aisle. When we reached the end, we turned and watched Papa and the minister come next. Then came Ben with Aunt Katherine on his arm. She looked so pretty I could hardly stand it. Jake stepped in from the edge to be next to Papa, and Mrs. Culshank came in from the other side, looking ready to hold up Aunt Katherine if she fainted or anything.

A number of ladies opened their pocketbooks and took out their hankies to dab at their eyes, I guess because Aunt Katherine was so happy and shy looking. Maybe they were thinking about Mama. I know I was. All the while we could hear the piano. Outside like that, the notes sounded small and thin. They seemed to drift up into the branches before our ears had a chance to catch them.

The minister said his words about how solemn the day was and how marrying someone is a serious step. I already knew that. Then he turned to Aunt Katherine and said for her to repeat after him.

"I, Katherine Suzanne Gilbert, take thee, Charles

August Hanson, to be my husband. . . ." She said all the *I do's* and *from this day forwards* and the *for better or for worses* and the *in sickness and in health* parts that the minister told her to say. She also said, "And I further give you my word, Charles, that I shall do my level best not to intrude on the privacy of the memories you have of my sister, your children's mother."

Next, it was Papa's turn. "I, Charles August Hanson, widower of Edna Gilbert Hanson, take thee, Katherine Suzanne Gilbert, to be my wife. . . ." He said the same *I do's* and *love, honor, and cherishes* that Aunt Katherine had repeated until the end, when he said, "And I further give you my word, Katherine, that I will do my level best neither to burden you with my sorrows nor to liken you to your sister in word or thought. I love you for your own sake and will do so forevermore."

Then they kissed on the lips and everyone clapped.

Ingrid's cake was perfect. Mrs. Culshank had put purple pansies all around the edge and Aunt Katherine had flavored the white icing with almond extract. Ingrid had made up an extra pan of cake ahead of time that Aunt Rosa cut into small cubes and tied into mesh bags with pink ribbons. These were put on a tray for girls and unmarried women to take home and put under their pillows in hopes of dreaming of the man they would marry someday.

Mrs. Breton was there. She told me I looked lovely in my new dress and that I was a very lucky girl to have such a nice family. I asked whether she still wanted pictures from me.

"Why, of course I do, Katy Sue," she said, and I laughed because she'd made a rhyme out of my name.

I rushed inside the house, through the kitchen and past all the relatives helping, to my room. Upstairs was quiet. The rest of the family was outside.

I went to my drawer where I keep special things. From it, I brought out all the pictures I'd been saving. Some were in crayon and some were in water paints, the ones Jake had left for me on my pillow. I'd tried a few times to use crayons and paints in the same picture, but it hadn't looked good, so I threw those away.

I brought out a picture of Mama sitting at the table where I'd put yellow stars around her and one where I had Mama side by side with Aunt Katherine. You could tell which was which because Aunt Katherine's hair was lighter and I'd drawn it in as shorter, although by then she'd let it grow. I even had one picture of Mama shaking hands with Alvin in front of our woodpile.

I had also painted a picture of a mother holding a baby. The baby was supposed to be me. Just then I had an idea, and set that one aside on my rug.

For my crow pictures, I'd used Jake's stuffed crow

as a model, like for where the eyes should go and how long the beaks would be. My best crow picture had nothing else in it except one bird standing sideways and looking forward. I imagined it was looking toward its chicks, only they weren't in the picture, because that was the easiest way for me to draw it. Ben had showed me how to use a blue crayon for the highlights. That made the feathers look blacker than if I'd just used black crayon and nothing else.

I took the picture of Papa and Ben and Ingrid and Mama and set it aside with the one of me as a baby where Aunt Katherine had me in the rocking chair. Then I chose the best crow picture and rolled the three together.

Back outside I found Jake visiting with a group of men. I took him by the hand and said, "I'd like you to meet my last year's teacher."

We walked into the orchard where Mrs. Breton was standing with her husband and Mrs. Harriman. When she turned away from the conversation, I stepped up to her and said, "Mrs. Breton? I'd like you to meet our friend, Hamilton Jacobs, and Jake, I'd like you to meet my teacher, Mrs. Breton."

They shook hands and said a few words about the weather, and Mrs. Breton said she'd known Jake's parents a long time ago.

Next, I pulled Mrs. Breton toward Aunt Katherine. They'd already met, of course. Mrs. Breton touched Aunt Katherine's new gold ring. When Uncle Dennis came up to ask Aunt Katherine something, Mrs. Breton and I were left standing there.

I fiddled with my roll of drawings. "I guess I have something for you, if you still want them," I said, and opened the roll. "Jake's the one who gave me the water paints. This picture here is of everyone in our family but me. See? I have them sitting on the porch—that porch right over there."

"That's lovely, dear," Mrs. Breton said.

"And, here. I have this picture of a crow. Remember? You asked if I could draw the crows. And you know what? I like crows now. Jake taught me that they're very intelligent and that they make better mothers than chickens do or almost any other bird you'd find on a farm."

"Gosh, Katy Sue," Mrs. Breton said, as she took the picture from me, "you've become quite an artist. Thank you."

Then I handed her the third picture. "And this one, too," I said. "This is supposed to be me when I was a baby. The woman is Aunt Katherine, who Papa said helped out when I was little and had the colic."

She took the picture and put it on top of the others. "That's lovely," she said.

"But the reason I thought you might like it is that I was thinking it could have been you with your own baby daughter," I said. "Way back when you still had her."

Mrs. Breton's eyes began to water.

"I hope I haven't hurt your feelings," I said, not knowing whether I'd done something wrong.

"Not at all, dear. Everyone cries at weddings these days." She looked off into the distance and then turned back to me. "You haven't hurt my feelings one bit," she said as she carefully rolled the three pictures so they'd fit in her handbag without getting squished too badly. She put her palm across my shoulders and guided me out of our orchard toward the cake table near the barn, where her husband was standing with some other men. "You've had a hard time out here on this farm," she said. "But someday, you'll learn what a lucky girl you are—a very lucky girl to know the things you know."

I didn't understand what Mrs. Breton had meant, but I was glad she had my pictures. I wondered what she'd do with them now that I'd finally given them to her. Some women hang kids' special drawings on their kitchen walls. I hoped she'd do that.

While everyone was laughing and visiting outside and having their strawberry punch, Uncle Dennis had gotten together with Jake to move Papa's things to the big bedroom upstairs. They'd pushed the furniture around into a new arrangement and carried the sewing machine in its case downstairs to our spare room, where Papa had been keeping himself. Next, they drove Uncle Dennis's Plymouth over to the Culshanks' and picked up the boxes and such that Aunt Katherine had packed up from the time she'd spent there.

Some of the cousins had started running around wild with their shirttails coming apart from their trousers, but by then it was time for everyone to return to their own lives.

Papa went around and thanked everybody for helping with the day. Finally, he hugged Jake good-bye and said, "Well, if we don't get going, how can anyone miss us?" and someone reminded him that he might as well arrive at the lodge early as late and that there were plenty of people to clean up, although Jake had to catch his train back home.

Papa put two satchels in the bed of our truck, his and Aunt Katherine's. He kissed Ben and Ingrid and me and Aunt Katherine did the same, reminding us that they'd be home by supper the next day and not to worry about missing church, since Ben would have no way to drive us. We'd never stayed in the house without a grown-up.

Papa started the truck in the middle of everyone waving to him and blowing kisses to Aunt Katherine and throwing rice. I ran after them as far as I could up our lane. Then they were gone. We don't know who it was, but at some point in the afternoon someone had sneaked up to our truck and tied a pair of old rubber boots to the back bumper. For a minute I could hear those boots drag against the blacktop of the county road after they turned west, and then nothing.

Uncle Dennis and Aunt Rosa were the last to leave. She and I ended up in the kitchen together, drying the plates. I'd taken off my wrist corsage and put it on the windowsill. I was thinking I'd ask the next day for help with pressing the flowers. I said, "When Papa and Aunt Katherine come home tomorrow—"

"I expect you'll be calling her Mama from here on out," Aunt Rosa said.

"I don't think so."

"But she's your stepmother, now."

"Yes, ma'am. I know," I said.

"Won't you want to be calling her Mama?"

"No, ma'am. She said she'll still be our aunt and that the way to be a good stepmother is not to try to be somebody's mother when you're not. My mama is Mama and Aunt Katherine is Aunt Katherine."

Aunt Rosa saw that her girls were roughhousing by the back steps. She rapped on the window glass to tell them to stop. Then she busied herself with getting plates back on the shelf.

"You get only one mama in this life," I said quietly.

I had grown tall enough to see out our kitchen window without standing on a stool. It was coming on toward late afternoon. The sky was blue as blue could be, the color of far away. It seemed almost to light up the new green of the linden tree and its branches on the horizon. I looked out there and hoped Mama agreed with how things had gone. Crows had come in and gathered around that tree. Maybe they were protecting it.

ABOUT THE AUTHOR

Ellie Mathews grew up on the wild edge of Puget Sound, where she has raised pigs, goats, sheep, and chickens. She is the author of young readers' fiction and adult nonfiction, for which she has received a variety of honors, including an arts commission award. She has one daughter and one granddaughter whose smile sends her over the moon. Mathews lives in the woods with her husband on the Olympic Peninsula, where it doesn't rain as much as everyone says.

If you enjoyed this book, you'll also want to read these other Milkweed novels.

To order books or for more information, contact Milkweed at (800) 520–6455 or visit our Web site (www.milkweed.org).

The $66 Summer
John Armistead
Milkweed Prize for Children's Literature
New York Public Library Best Books of the Year: "Books for the Teen Age"
A story of interracial friendships in the segregation-era South.

Runt
V. M. Caldwell
A twelve-year-old boy forges an unusual friendship while dealing with the death of his mother.

Alligator Crossing
Marjory Stoneman Douglas
Features the wildlife of the Everglades just before it was declared a national park.

Perfect
Natasha Friend
Milkweed Prize for Children's Literature
A thirteen-year-old girl struggles with bulimia after her father dies.

The Trouble with Jeremy Chance
George Harrar
Bank Street College Best Children's Books of the Year
Father-son conflict during the final days of World War I.

No Place
Kay Haugaard
Based on a true story of Latino youth who create an inner-city park.

I Am Lavina Cumming
Susan Lowell
Mountains & Plains Booksellers Association Award
This lively story culminates with the 1906 San Francisco earthquake.

A Small Boat at the Bottom of the Sea
John Thomson
A twelve-year-old's summer with his aunt and uncle on Puget Sound tests his convictions.

Behind the Bedroom Wall
Laura E. Williams
Milkweed Prize for Children's Literature
Jane Addams Peace Award Honor Book
Tells a story of the Holocaust through the eyes of a young girl.

MILKWEED EDITIONS

Founded in 1979, Milkweed Editions is one of the largest independent, nonprofit literary publishers in the United States. Milkweed publishes with the intention of making a humane impact on society, in the belief that great writing can transform the human heart and spirit. Within this mission, Milkweed publishes in four areas: fiction, nonfiction, poetry, and children's literature for middle-grade readers.

JOIN US

Milkweed depends on the generosity of foundations and individuals like you, in addition to the sales of its books. In an increasingly consolidated and bottom-line-driven publishing world, your support allows us to select and publish books on the basis of their literary quality and the depth of their message. Please visit our Web site (www.milkweed.org) or contact us at (800) 520-6455 to learn more about our donor program.

Interior design by Dorie McClelland
Typeset in Adobe Garamond Pro
by Dorie McClelland
Printed on acid-free Glatfelter paper
by Friesens Corporation